ARMY OF 12 MONKEYS

When she looked up, Cole was standing there above her in the blue-tinged darkness. He no longer looked merely insane, or even dangerous. With his bloody face, eyes staring grimly at her, and the cheap pistol gripped in his immense hand, he looked positively lethal.

"Are you hurt?" he asked, shoving the gun into a pocket. He sounded as though it pained him to talk.

Kathryn stumbled to her feet. "Uh, no. Yes—" She glanced down quickly at her torn skirt, blood threading along the cuffs of her blouse.

He wasn't listening.

He pulled her down the hall, past another lurid crimson circle with its crude grinning monkeys. Ahead of them a faint glimmer of light showed through the murk, giving a sanguine glow to the trail of spattered red paint that stretched before them.

"You didn't have a gun before, did you?" Kathryn asked, her voice dead.

"I've got one now," Cole replied, and dragged her toward the light.

12 Monkeys

A novel by
Elizabeth Hand

BASED ON AN ORIGINAL SCREENPLAY BY
DAVID PEOPLES & JANET PEOPLES

HarperPrism
An Imprint of HarperPaperbacks

This is a work of fiction. The characters, incidents, and dialogues are products of the author's imagination and are not to be construed as real. Any resemblance to actual events or persons, living or dead, is entirely coincidental.

HarperPaperbacks   *A Division of* HarperCollins*Publishers*
10 East 53rd Street, New York, N.Y. 10022

First printing: December 1995

Printed in the United States of America

HarperPrism is an imprint of HarperPaperbacks.
HarperPaperbacks, HarperPrism, and colophon are trademarks of HarperCollins*Publishers*.

❖ 10 9 8 7 6 5 4 3 2 1

12 Monkeys

Nothing sorts out memories from
   ordinary moments.
It is only later that they claim remembrance,
   when they show their scars.

CHRIS MARKER,
"La Jetée"

In the dream there is thunder, people shouting, the muted hissing of an intercom. High overhead a monitor displays flight times, a picture of smiling children. Twenty yards away a woman kneels on the tiled floor beside a man in a flowered shirt. As the boy watches them, his mother's hand tightens around his. He can smell his father's sweat, overpowering his Old Spice aftershave, hear his father's voice breaking as he yanks him roughly away.

"Come on . . . "

Then the clatter of running feet, the distant high-pitched beeping of an alarm somewhere in the airport. He stares, refusing to budge, and wrinkles his nose. There is a smell at once oddly familiar yet strange, something he is certain he has never smelled before: salt and scorched metal. For an instant he wonders if it is a dream, has he perhaps forgotten something? But then his father's voice grows angry, even frightened.

". . . come on, this is no place for us."

As his parents hurry him away, he cranes his head,

still transfixed by the kneeling woman. Her spun-candy hair glowing beneath the fluorescent lights, her mouth open as though to receive a kiss, but he thinks no, she is about to scream. . . .

But she doesn't. Instead her head dips toward the man's. Even from here he can see tears welling, a small black streak of mascara. The man sprawled on the floor lifts his hand. He touches her, his fingers leaving small red blooms upon her cheek. Then his hand falls limply across his chest, where more flowers bloom, lush and moist, staining the gaudy Hawaiian shirt red.

"Flight 784 for San Francisco is now ready for boarding," the PA announces. *"Gate number thirty-eight, gate number . . . "*

People are everywhere now. Someone helps the woman to her feet; someone else crouches beside the man on the floor and frantically tears his Hawaiian shirt open. In the distance the boy hears a siren, shouting, the crackle of a security walkie-talkie. His father pulls him roughly around a corner. His mother's hand nestles in his hair and he can hear her murmuring, more to herself than to him—

"It's okay, don't worry, it's all going to be okay. . . . "

But even then he knew she was lying, that nothing was ever going to be okay again. Even then, he knew he had watched a man die.

He awoke in near-darkness, as he always did. The smells of aftershave and salt faded into a warm stench of unwashed bodies and excrement. Overhead an intercom blared between bursts of static.

" . . . number 5429, Ishigura. Number 87645, Cole . . . "

He blinked, confused, running a hand across his face and pushing his lank dark hair from his eyes. "Number 87645 . . . " At the sound of his own number Cole grimaced into full wakefulness, glanced at the bunk cage next to his.

"Hey," he whispered. "Jose! What's going on?"

In the other cages people twisted to look at him, their eyes glittering in the dim light. For a moment Jose refused to meet his gaze.

Then, "They said your name, man," he whispered.

Cole shook his head. "I was asleep," he said. "I was dreaming."

"Too bad you woke up." Jose turned onto his stomach, his elbow grazing the bunk's metal grille. "They're lookin' for volunteers."

A chill snaked across Cole's neck. "Volunteers," he repeated numbly. From the darkened corridor voices echoed, the clatter of boots on broken concrete. Jose bared his teeth in a grin.

"Hey, maybe they'll give you a pardon, man."

"Sure," said Cole. His whole body was cold now, sweat breaking out beneath the thin rough fabric of his uniform. "That's why 'volunteers' never come back; they all get pardoned."

The voices grew closer. From the metal bunks came the scrape of skin against steel as people twisted and groped for a better vantage point. "Some guys come back," Jose said hopefully. "That's what I heard."

"You mean up on seven?" Cole bared his teeth

and thrust a thumb at the low ceiling. "Hiding 'em up there. All messed up in the head. Brains gone. Crazy."

"You don't know they're all messed up," Jose said a little desperately. "You ain't seen 'em. Nobody's seen 'em. Maybe they're not messed up. That's just a rumor. Nobody knows that." His gaze grew dreamy, unfocused. "I don't believe that," he insisted in a soft voice.

A glare sliced through the darkness, flashlight beams moving across shaven scalps, mouths with missing teeth. Jose yanked the covers over his face.

"Good luck, man," he hissed.

Cole blinked as a corona of brilliant light stopped in front of his cage.

"Volunteer duty," a heavyset guard announced.

"I didn't volunteer," Cole said in a low voice. In the other bunks prisoners watched through narrowed eyes.

"You causing trouble again?" the guard snarled.

Cole stared at him, then shook his head. "No trouble," he murmured. "No trouble at all."

The cage's tiny door swung open and Cole scrambled out, the guards grabbing his arms and pulling him roughly to the floor. He walked between them, trying not to see the hundreds of eyes fixed on him, cold and bright as steel bearings, trying not to hear the low epithets and guttural curses, the occasional whispered "Good luck, man," that followed him through the filthy hallway.

Volunteer duty . . .

They took him to a part of the compound he had

never been in before, walking past endless ranks of cages, through endless corridors without windows or doors. The putrid odor of the bunks dissipated, replaced by stale warm air. The halls grew wider. Doors appeared, most of them yawning into utter darkness. After about fifteen minutes, they stopped in front of a metal wall scabbed with rust and myriad bullet holes.

"Here." The guard who had first spoken punched in an access code. The door opened and the guard pushed him inside. Cole lurched forward, tripping so that he fell to the floor. With a muted *shhh* the door closed behind him.

He didn't know how long he lay there, listening to his heartbeat, the sound of the guard's footsteps echoing into silence. When at last he tried to stand his legs ached, as though unaccustomed to moving. There was a bitter taste in the back of his mouth. He was in a room so dark he could make out only shadows, the angular bulk of machinery and coils of wire, and what looked like pipes hanging from the ceiling.

"Proceed," a voice commanded. Cole looked around until he found its source, a tiny grate in a wall.

"Proceed what?" he demanded.

"Proceed," the voice repeated, this time with a hint of menace.

Cole carefully walked across the dim room, trying not to stumble. He had almost reached the far side when he halted, holding his breath.

Against the wall loomed a line of pale figures, ghostlike, their eyes huge and blank. Cole stared at them, then let his breath out in a sigh of relief: they were neither ghosts nor interrogators but suits. Space suits, or contamination suits, each with a helmet and plastic visor. Beneath them were rows of oxygen tanks, boxes containing flashlights, plastic tubes and bottles, heavy industrial gloves, maps.

"Proceed," the voice from the grate repeated.

He fumbled through the suits until he found one that looked as though it might fit. He shrugged it on, the material pulling snugly across his barrel chest, then struggled with the zipper.

"All openings must be closed," the voice said. Cole tugged at the zipper, wincing as the metal teeth bit at his chest. "If the integrity of the suit is compromised in any way, if the fabric is torn or a zipper not closed, readmittance will be denied." More zippers, a series of metal clasps. Then he stood there, breathing hard, already sweating in his heavy fabric shell.

"Proceed," the voice commanded.

He looked around and saw another, smaller, door in the wall behind him. He started for it, stopped. He flipped the plastic helmet over his head, adjusting the visor, then bent and hefted one of the oxygen tanks. "Jesus," he muttered, grunting as he slung it onto his back. He pulled the tubing from its casing and threaded it through his helmet. Then he stooped before the box at his feet, taking out first one object and then another, staring at them and frowning. As though in a dream he held up a bottle, squinting to see if it had a label, then replaced it and grabbed a larger one. The bitter taste in his throat grew more pronounced and he yawned, covering his mouth with a gloved hand. Bottles, vials, a map. Last of all he dug out a flashlight, testing it to make sure it worked.

"Proceed."

Cole crossed the room, slowly and awkwardly in the heavy suit, his heart pounding with exertion and what he refused to recognize as fear. When he reached the door it slid open, revealing a tiny chamber, a kind of air lock. He stepped inside. The door boomed shut behind him. His breath came more quickly as he sucked oxygen from the air tanks on his back. On the opposite wall of the chamber was another door with a huge wheel lock. He turned the wheel, groaning at its weight, then slowly pushed the door open and stepped through. Immediately he lost his balance, catching himself before he hit the floor.

"Son of a bitch."

The entire room shuddered. There was a grinding sound, a series of deafening clanks: he was inside an ascending elevator. For several minutes he leaned against the wall, trying to calm himself. Then the elevator jolted to a stop. Cole stepped hesitantly back to the door. A minute passed; neither elevator nor door moved. His own breath thundered in his ears. Finally he braced himself and slowly pulled the door open.

Outside unbroken darkness streamed. He could hear the soft *plink plink* of water dripping, muffled by his helmet. His flashlight showed black water moving sluggishly through a wide underground channel. A sewer. Cole felt a twinge of gratitude for his oxygen tank. A few yards away a rusted ladder straddled a crumbling concrete wall. Cole fumbled at his belt until he found his map, unfolding it awkwardly with his gloved hands. He looked back at the ladder, with a sigh refolded the map, and sloshed out into the channel.

The ladder shuddered beneath him as he climbed, trying to shift his weight evenly so that the whole ramshackle construction didn't send him crashing into the black water below. Once he almost lost the flashlight. When at last he reached the top step his head bumped against the ceiling, the cracked concrete slimed with black, trailing streamers of mold. Cole grimaced, peering up until he found what he was looking for. He clutched at the ladder with one hand, with the other pushed against the ceiling until it trembled. With a sudden sharp creak the manhole cover gave way. A circle of bluish light opened above him as he shoved it aside. He clambered out.

Night!

But not the artificial night he had known for so long, with its stench of caged men and decaying vegetable protein. Instead, above him loomed buildings, townhouses and skyscrapers and brick tenements, their broken windows like silver teeth glowing in the moonlight. Silver fell through the air as well; he held out one gloved hand and watched in amazement as it was dusted with crystal.

Snow. *Snow!*

"Sweet Jesus," he murmured.

Real cold. Real snow.

He straightened, turning so that his flashlight swept across the landscape. He was in a square surrounded by dead buildings, immense trees whose limbs crowded empty storefronts, the crumpled spines of telephone poles. Vine-covered humps of metal that he knew must be automobiles. He couldn't recall when he had last seen an automobile, but at sight of the vines he frowned, remembering something. Another dream: this one of a room filled with light, a circle of white faces and a monotonous voice reciting as images flickered across a screen.

"*Pueraria lobata*, common kudzu. A noxious plant that serves as host to a variety of insects. . . ."

He groped at his belt until he found a bottle, then cautiously approached the cars. With one hand he dug among the vines, until with a cry of triumph he captured a tiny wood beetle. Clumsily he popped the top of the collection tube and was dropping the beetle inside when something rustled behind him. Balancing the tube against his chest, he turned.

"What the—!"

In the flashlight's glare an enormous creature reared, snarling. Cole stumbled backward; the creature remained poised before him, clawing at the drifting snow, its mouth open to show rows of white teeth.

"Jesus!"

A bear. The snarl became a roar. For a moment Cole thought it was going to lunge at him. Instead it abruptly sank onto all fours, turned, and without a backward glance padded down the street. Cole watched it go, his heart thundering. When it was out of sight he walked slowly into the square.

The moonlight made a frozen circus of store windows adrift with snow and dead leaves. In one, a toy train set lay in pieces. Blank-eyed mannequins wore rags and bits of tinsel, their rigid hands pointing at stuffed toys oozing shredded foam and sawdust. Beneath a tipsy metal Christmas tree lay a fallen angel, her face pocked with dirt. Carefully Cole stepped through the broken window and walked up and down the aisles, his flashlight playing across crumpled metal racks filled with rotting clothes. He stopped when the light struck a mannequin wearing a Hawaiian shirt, grinning maniacally beneath a sign that proclaimed: START THE NEW YEAR IN THE KEYS!!! Between the mannequin's outstretched hands an elaborate spiderweb glimmered in the flashlight's gleam.

"Okay." Cole breathed, reaching for another collection bottle. As his gloved hand reached and plucked at the spider, the web collapsed. With a sound like a sigh, the mannequin shivered. The Hawaiian shirt turned to dust as pigeons fluttered overhead, roosting in the shadows.

He went back outside, broken glass crunching beneath his feet. Snow blew in soft eddies against the sides of empty buildings. In the distance he heard a faint howling: wolves. At the end of the square there was a movie theater. On the sidewalk beneath the marquee stray letters lay beneath a dusting of snow. Overhead the marquee read:

F LM CLAS ICS 24 HRS/HIT HCOCK ESTIVAL

He barely registered the marquee, instead moved slowly and purposefully toward the crumbling brick wall that stretched beside it. Amidst obscene graffiti and tattered posters there was a stenciled image: twelve monkeys dancing in a closed circle. Beside it were the words: WE DID IT!

Cole stared at the stencil. When he swallowed his mouth tasted sour, with a bitter aftertaste. He turned from the wall and continued out of the square, passing a vast deserted train station. He did not see the crouching figures in the station's yawning entrance—six wolves, their green eyes glowing balefully in the moonlight. But there were other, solitary footprints there, very large, with pronounced claws at the tips of each toe pad. He followed these, until he saw at his feet a small brown mound steaming in the cold. Cole bent and scooped some of the feces into another collection tube. Behind him the wolves slipped silently away, disappearing behind an abandoned baby carriage. Cole replaced the top of the collection tube and continued to follow the animal's tracks.

Further on he came to a beautiful old beaux arts building extravagantly overgrown with ivy, its broken steps littered with bones and broken glass. The footprints led here, up the steps and inside a darkened archway. High up on the building's rococo exterior an owl perched, its round, yellow gaze fixed upon the man below. Pale streamers of light washed across the building's steps. As Cole passed through the arched entryway, the owl blinked at the rind of sunlight showing above the horizon. Then it spread its wings and lifted high into the air above the deserted city.

The footsteps led through a huge lobby overgrown with trees. From a broken skylight high above pale sun trickled. There were drifts of leaves everywhere, and an animal odor so pungent that Cole could smell it even through his visor. He passed massive columns entwined with vines, wide marble steps slick with ice and rotting vegetation. He climbed the stairs, panting a little now, until he reached the very top of the building. Wide doorways led out onto a viewing deck. Broken slates and glass were everywhere. Warily he followed the footsteps out there, trudging through the debris. There was a small coughing sound, like someone clearing his throat. Cole whirled.

On the wall behind him a circle was stenciled in red paint. Within it twelve monkeys danced and grinned above the same triumphant legend.

WE DID IT!!!

The coughing sound came again, louder this time. Cole lifted his head and saw up on the roof of the ornate building a silhouette, black against the sudden glory of sunrise. A lion, its mane a brilliant corona of gold as it threw its head back and roared until the air rang with the sound—sole ruler of a kingdom abandoned by men.

"Proceed."

Freezing water roared from nozzles in the wall, pummeling Cole's naked body. He shivered, trying not to cry out, and ducked as two hulking figures in decontamination suits stabbed at him with two long poles. The poles ended in stiff wire brushes. The figures poked at him mercilessly; every now and then he could glimpse one smiling through the suit's smudged mask.

"Raise your arms above your head."

Cole obeyed, wincing as the water was replaced by caustic chemicals that burned his skin. The suited figures began scrubbing at his armpits. Foul-smelling water sluiced around his ankles and whorled down the drain. From a grate overhead a voice commanded:

"Proceed."

The two figures stepped away. Shuddering, Cole walked from the shower and down a narrow passage, still naked, every inch of him feeling raw. In the next room a three-legged stool stood beneath a single flickering light. Beside the stool was a small white plastic box. Cole grit his teeth to keep them from chattering and sat down.

"Proceed."

The stool groaned beneath his weight as he reached for the white plastic box and withdrew an old-fashioned hypodermic needle. He made a fist, clumsily jabbing at his arm and watching blood move slowly up the syringe's neck. When he glanced up he saw a single, nearly opaque window of thick plastic in the rusty iron wall. Behind it shadowy figures moved, watching him. When the syringe was full he replaced it gingerly in a compartment in the plastic box. In the narrow doorway two guards appeared, holding a prison uniform. Without waiting for the command Cole stood, walked over to them, and dressed.

When he was done, they escorted him along a walkway in the cavernous underground space. The uniform chafed painfully at his skin. The air smelled stale, but not as warm as it did in the prisoners' quarters. He didn't make the mistake of asking his guards where they were taking him. After some minutes, they stopped in front of a tall door that slid open silently.

"Go." One of the guards shoved Cole forward.

He was inside a chamber where every conceivable surface was covered with print: walls and ceiling, even parts of the floor were papered with photographs, old newspapers, maps and charts, computer readouts, traffic tickets, magazine covers, surgeon's reports, handbills. "CLOCK STILL TICKING!!! NO CURE YET!!!" one headline screamed. Warped bookshelves sank beneath the weight of moldering volumes, incomplete sets of encyclopedias. Against one wall stood a bank of computers, their screens blank and gray. There was a makeshift pyramid of televisions with broken screens, an ancient Motorola radio. In the center of all this stretched a long conference table littered with even more technological debris—computer circuitry, a few dozen television remote control units, a transistor radio. Around the table sat six men and women in stained white clothes that reminded Cole of surgical scrubs.

One of the guards cleared his throat. "James Cole. Cleared from quarantine," he announced.

At the head of the table a man with delicate, rather jaded features and long pale hands nodded. He wore a pair of heavy dark square-framed glasses. "Thank you. You may wait outside," he said to the guards. His dark glasses fixed on Cole appraisingly.

"He's got a history, Doctor," the other guard warned. "Violence. Antisocial Six, doing twenty-five to life."

The scientist's blank gaze remained on Cole. "I don't think he's going to hurt us. You're not going to hurt us, are you, Mr. Cole?"

Cole shook his head imperceptibly. "No, sir."

"Of course not. Prisoners are not in the habit of harming innocent microbiologists like myself." He smiled coldly, then made a dismissive gesture at the guards. "You may go. Why don't you sit down, Mr. Cole?"

There was an empty chair at the conference table. Cole glanced around at the others. They regarded him coolly, impersonally; one woman stifled a yawn.

"Mr. Cole?" the microbiologist urged softly. Cole sat.

The man made a temple of his fingers. For several minutes he said nothing. Then, "We want you to tell us about last night."

Cole took a breath. "There's not much to tell," he began. "I—"

"No," the microbiologist corrected him. His voice was light, menacing. "We will ask you questions. You will answer in as much detail as possible. So: when you first left the elevator, where did you find yourself?"

"In a sewer."

"A sewer." The microbiologist glanced at the woman next to him, who was scribbling earnestly on a torn bit of paper. "In what direction was the water flowing?"

Cole frowned. "In what—"

"No questions, Mr. Cole!" the microbiologist snapped, showing even, white teeth. "You must observe everything. Again, in what direction was the water flowing?"

"Uh . . . north," Cole said, guessing. He felt sweat begin to pearl on his forehead.

"North," the microbiologist repeated, adjusting his dark glasses. Several of the others nodded. "Very good. Now, did you notice anything in the water?"

It went on like that for an hour. Cole's eyes watered from exhaustion; the acrid chemical taste coated his tongue. Another scientist handed him a blackboard and asked him to sketch a map.

"Sample number four. Where did you find that?"

Cole fidgeted in his seat. The room swam before his eyes; his fingers left damp smudges on the blackboard. "Uh . . ."

"It's important to observe everything," a woman broke in impatiently.

Cole swallowed. "I think it was . . . I'm sure it was Second Street."

The scientists began to whisper excitedly among themselves. Cole started to yawn, clapped a hand over his mouth. He looked around the room, finally focusing on another headline.

"VIRUS MUTATING!!!"

Beside it was a faded newspaper photograph of an old man in a tweed jacket, an expression of resigned despair on his chiseled features.

"SCIENTIST SAYS, 'IT'S TOO LATE FOR CURE.'"

A voice shattered Cole's reverie. "Close your eyes, Cole." Cole started, then obediently shut his eyes. The darkness was a blessed relief.

"Tell us in detail what you've seen in this room," a woman said softly.

Cole shook his head. "In this room? Uh . . . "

"Tell us about the pictures on the wall," the micro-biologist said.

"You mean the newspapers?"

"That's right," the woman said soothingly. "Tell us about the newspapers, Cole. Can you hear my voice? What does he look like, the man who just spoke? How old were you when you first left the surface?"

"How old . . . ?"

"Tell us," she urged.

"Tell us," other voices chimed in. "Tell us, tell us . . . "

He tilted his head back, eyes still tightly shut, his body aching with exhaustion. The bitter taste lingered in the back of his throat. He wondered vaguely if he had been drugged—he could remember so little, even now he was uncertain if he was awake or dreaming. *How old were you when you left the surface?* He tried not to yawn as the voices blurred and faded into another voice, droning on and on. . . .

"Flight 784 is now boarding at Gate . . . "

He stood in front of the observation window, watching as a 737 descended smoothly through the smoggy air, then touched down onto the runway, tires shrieking. His mother's hand held his loosely. His father pointed at the aircraft and said, "Look—there it is—"

From behind them came a shout, then a woman's voice, yelling. He turned, his father grabbing his free hand, and saw a middle-aged man with a thinning ponytail hurrying past. As the man turned the corner, he bumped the young Cole with a Chicago Bulls sports bag.

"Hey." Cole frowned at the man's departing back. A woman's voice pierced the air.

"NOOOOOO!"

Everywhere there were people running and screaming, luggage skidding across the floor as they fled. Cole watched open-mouthed as a man dove to the floor, arching onto his back and staring up at Cole with panicky eyes as he cried—

"Just exactly why did you volunteer?"

Cole gasped. His eyes flew open: he saw before him the long litter-strewn table ringed with anxious faces.

"I said, why did you volunteer?" The microbiologist impatiently tapped a pencil on the table.

Cole swallowed, looked around. "Well, uh—actually, the guard woke me up. He told me I volunteered."

The scientists turned to each other, whispering urgently. Cole tried desperately to keep his eyes open, but it was too much: the dream started to take him again. His head dropped, he could hear an intercom blaring, and footsteps . . .

"Cole? Cole?"

Once more the tapping sound pushed him into wakefulness. Cole started, gazing into the eyes of an earnest-looking man with silver hair and one gold earring—an astrophysicist, he had told Cole earlier. The astrophysicist nodded as he went on, "We appreciate your volunteering. You're a very good observer, Cole."

Cole glanced over at the microbiologist, his pencil drumming its tattoo on the tabletop. He nodded. "Uh, thank you."

"You'll get a reduction in sentence." The silver-haired astrophysicist looked at Cole, obviously waiting for him to thank him again, but Cole kept his face impassive.

"To be determined by the proper authorities," another scientist broke in.

"We have another program," a zoologist added. It was clear from her tone that she expected Cole to be impressed by this. "Very advanced, something quite different. Requires very skilled people."

The microbiologist leaned across the table, his dark glasses pointing ominously to Cole. "It would be an opportunity to reduce your sentence considerably. . . . "

The zoologist nodded. "And possibly play an important role in returning the human race to the surface of the earth," she said.

"We want tough-minded people. Strong mentally." The earnest-looking astrophysicist tugged at his earring, then glanced at the man beside him. "We've had some—misfortunes—with unstable types."

Cole felt a tightening in his stomach. One of the women gazed pointedly at him. "For a man in your position," she said, her eyes glinting, "this could be an opportunity."

"Not to volunteer could be a real mistake," a man added softly.

Cole opened his mouth to reply, hesitated. The microbiologist tapped his pencil impatiently.

"Definitely a mistake," he said.

Cole stared at the pencil, the thin pale fingers that clutched it, then looked around the table at the ring of anxious faces. He took a deep breath and asked, "When do I begin?"

"Yet among the myriad microwaves, the infrared messages, the gigabytes of ones and zeroes, we find words, byte-sized now . . . "

Dr. Kathryn Railly stared raptly at the man perched on a high stool at the front of the room. She'd heard him read before, at another club in Philly, but tonight he was really on a roll. She adjusted her glasses, brushed a strand of dark hair from her elegantly composed face, and leaned forward, listening intently.

" . . . words, tinier even than science, lurking in some vague electricity where, if we listen, we can still hear the solitary voice of that poet telling us, 'Yesterday This Day's Madness Did Prepare; Tomorrow's Silence, Triumph or Despair . . . '"

Breep! Breep!

Kathryn started, then reached reflexively for the beeper in her pocket. From their chairs, several black-clad bohos glanced at her and scowled.

"Sorry," she whispered, and stood. Her neighbors shot her filthy looks as she stepped over their feet, picking her way through folding chairs and coffee mugs and nouveaux beatniks. "'Scuse me, sorry . . . "

From his seat the poet glared at her, his voice

rising. "'. . . for you know not why you go, nor where . . .'"

Only, of course, Kathryn did know "where." In the lobby she found a pay phone and made a quick call. A second call sent her to the Eighth Precinct Station House. Detective Franki met her in the hallway. He was a man on the young side of forty, with eyes that had seen too many greasy dawns on the wrong side of town. He nodded at her briefly.

"Dr. Railly. Thanks." Without further ado, he took her arm, propelling her down the corridor as he filled her in on the case.

" . . . so they get there, they ask the guy real nice for some kind of ID. He gets agitated and starts screaming about viruses. Totally irrational, totally disoriented, doesn't know where he is, doesn't know what day it is, the whole ball of wax. All they got was his name." Franki shoved a paper at Kathryn as they strode past crowded holding cells. "They figure he's stoned out of his mind, or it's some kind of psychotic episode, so—"

"He's been tested for drugs?"

Franki shook his head. "Negative for drugs. But he took on five cops like he was dusted to the eyeballs. No drugs! You believe that?"

He paused in front of a tiny observation window. Kathryn took a breath, trying not to wince at the rank scents of urine and disinfectant. Then she leaned forward and peered through the dirty glass.

Inside the padded cell a man was restrained to a heavy steel chair. He was of average height but powerfully built, with smoothly muscled forearms and neck, high forehead, and a prizefighter's nose. His hair was a black stubble across his scalp, his eyes blearily alert as he stared at the gray walls. Sweat trickled down his forehead, threading between bruises and welts, and a nasty-looking cut above one eyebrow. Every now and then his head would start to droop forward, as though he were falling asleep, until the restraints grew taut and he jerked upright again to stare wide-eyed at the empty room.

"You have him in restraints," Kathryn Railly said in a low voice.

"Were you listening?" Franki punched the wall in frustration. "We got two officers in the hospital! Yeah, he's in restraints, plus the medic gave him enough Stelazine to kill a horse! Look at him! Raring to go!"

Kathryn sighed. The man looked more like he was ready to pass out. As she watched, his head swiveled, slowly, until he was staring directly at her. His eyes narrowed, giving him a ferociously intense look. Kathryn found herself backing away slightly from the window.

"That would explain the bruises, I guess," she said. "The struggle."

Franki sighed. "Yeah, yeah. You want to go in? Examine him?"

"Yes, please." She glanced at the page in her hand. "This is all you have on him? You ran it through the system?"

"No match up." A click as Franki unlocked the door. "No license, no prints, no warrants. Nothing. I should probably go in with you."

She stepped around him and into the cell. "Thank you, but that won't be necessary."

Franki watched her, nodding. "Well, I'll be right here. Just in case."

She crossed the cell, moving confidently but with care, always mindful of the door behind her. "Mr. Cole?" she said warmly. "My name is Dr. Railly—"

The gaze he turned on her was as innocent and beatific as a child's—or a lunatic's. She felt a small spark of unease, recalling Detective Franki's words: *No drugs. You believe that?* She cleared her throat and went on.

"I'm a psychiatrist, Mr. Cole. I work for the county. I don't work for the police. My concern is your well-being. Can you tell me what happened this evening?"

The man stared at her, unblinking. "I need to go now." His voice was low and unthreatening, almost soothing, as though she were the one in trouble. Kathryn tilted her head, nodding.

"Mr. Cole. I'm not going to lie to you. I can't make the police let you go. But I will try and help you—if you cooperate. Can you do that, James?" She glanced at the page in her hand. "May I call you James?"

"James!" The man snorted. "Nobody ever calls me that."

Kathryn frowned. "Have you been a patient at County? Have I seen you someplace?"

He shook his head, the restraints biting into the bruised skin of his neck. "No, not possible." He sounded more agitated; his gaze flickered nervously from Kathryn to the door to the observation window. "I . . . I have to get out of here. S'posed to be getting information."

Mood lability, apprehension, possible hostile paranoia, thought Kathryn. She nodded sympathetically and asked, "What kind of information?"

"It won't help you. You can't do anything about it. You can't change anything."

"Change what?"

Cole's voice rose. "I need to go."

Definite hostility and poor frustration tolerance. Kathryn slapped the paper against her palm. "Do you know why you're here, James?"

"Yes. I'm a good observer—I have a tough mind."

"I see. You don't remember assaulting a police officer? Several officers?"

"They wanted identification," said Cole. "I don't have any identification. I wasn't trying to hurt them."

"You don't have a driver's license, James? Or a Social Security card?"

"No."

Kathryn hesitated, noting possible side effects of the Stelazine: facial muscle spasms, those nervous glances that might be indicative of blurred vision. "You've been in an institution, haven't you, James? A hospital?"

"I have to go."

"In jail? Prison?"

Cole sighed resignedly. "Underground."

"Hiding?"

He gazed up at her. Once more his expression grew childlike. "I love this air," he said softly. For the first time he smiled. It made him look sweet, boyish. "This is wonderful air."

Kathryn ventured a half-smile in return. "What's wonderful about the air, James?"

"It's so clean and fresh. And no germs!"

"Why do you think there aren't any germs in the air, James?"

He went on as though he hadn't heard her. "This is October, right?"

She shook her head. "April."

"April?"

"What year do you think it is, James?"

"1996."

"You think it's 1996?" Kathryn asked, her voice steady. *Delusional, possibly hallucinating.* "That's the future, James. Do you think you're living in the future?"

Cole's expression clouded into bewilderment. "No, 1996 is the past."

"1996 is the future, James," she said calmly. "This is 1990."

He looked up at her, too stunned to speak. For a moment Kathryn gazed at him, taking in those impossibly deep eyes—incredulous now, almost desperate. "Thank you, James," she said at last, and turning she strode quickly to the door. Detective Franki held it open for her.

"Well?" he demanded.

"He's certainly delusional," she said, sighing. "Maybe even mildly schizophrenic. Hard to tell when all you can see is his face, and that's been beaten black-and-blue." She shot Franki an icy look. "Oh, I know: 'potential cop killer in a major psychotic episode.' But it'd sure make my job easier if you hadn't tranked him up so much I can't make a valid diagnosis."

Franki rolled his eyes. "Yeah, yeah. You gonna sign or what?"

"Oh, I'll sign," she said coolly. She followed him to his desk and filled out a set of forms. "Seventy-two hours observation, some more drug testing. If he lands on the street again, I hope it's not in your jurisdiction."

Franki smiled. "Me, too. Thanks, Dr. Railly."

She stood to go, brushing a tendril of hair from her eyes. At the door she paused. "Oh, and Detective Franki—it's difficult to make impartial judgments when you're so obviously stressed."

He snorted. "Yeah, well, I could use a fucking vacation."

"I was thinking more like Prozac," she said sweetly. "Think about it." And she left.

In his cell, Cole blinked and stared dazedly at the padded gray wall, the tiny lozenge of thick glass where shadowy figures came and went. The bitter taste in his mouth was so strong now that he almost gagged. He tried to focus on something besides rising nausea and the painful throbbing above his left eye. Had there been a woman here, asking questions? Or was that another nightmare, like the one with the scientists? He licked his lips, tasting blood and bile, and looked up when he heard the door grinding open again. Two surly policemen entered. One roughly undid the restraints that bound him to the chair. The other knelt and clapped a pair of heavy manacles about Cole's ankles.

"C'mon," he snapped, yanking Cole to his feet.

"Where you taking me?" Cole asked thickly as he lurched forward.

One of the policemen reached over to tighten the straitjacket. "South of France, buddy. Fancy hotel. You're gonna love it."

Cole jerked his head back. "South of France! I don't want to go to the south of France." He frowned, ragged bits of memory—or was it a dream?—coming back to him. "I want to—to make a telephone call."

The policeman smirked as he led him from the cell. "Zip it, ace. You fooled the shrink with your act, but you don't fool us."

Cole stumbled down the hall between them until they stopped in front of a steel door. One of the policemen unlocked it. A moment later the door swung out. Cole blinked, amazed, as morning overwhelmed him, a dazzling fury of white light.

"Send us a postcard, okay, ace?" The policeman laughed as he led Cole into the waiting prison van.

"Yeah," the other cop sneered, holding the door open for his colleague. "Don't forget to write."

Cole stared blankly as the door clanged shut. With a muted roar, the van pulled into the city street.

When the van finally stopped, someone came and removed the manacles. Someone else dragged him, less roughly this time, into another grim building. There were more gray corridors, another white-tiled room. Two attendants stripped him, tossing the strait-jacket into a metal bin, then arranged him beneath an institutional shower. Cole stood there obediently, gri-macing as the hot water raced across his bruised face and chest. One of the orderlies turned off the water. The other, a broad-shouldered man whose ID tag read BILLINGS, handed Cole a towel.

"C'mere," he said, his fingers digging into Cole's scalp. "Lemme see your head, Jimbo, see if you got any creepy-crawlies."

Cole stared dumbly at the towel, then looked up at Billings. "I need to make a telephone call."

"Gotta work that out with a doctor, Jimbo." The orderly's hands kneaded Cole's forehead. "Can't make no calls till the doctor says."

Cole's eyes flashed. "It's very important."

Billings drew back, but his hands remained on Cole's scalp. "Whatcha gotta do, Jimbo, is take it easy, relax into things." His fingers tightened until Cole's eyes burned with tears. "We all gonna get along fine, if you just relax."

Cole gasped with pain. Billings watched him, then finally withdrew his hands. "That's better," he said, smiling. "Now let's get you some clothes, Jimbo, introduce you to your new pals."

He stood while they dressed him in brown polyester trousers and a cheap Orlon shirt. "Nice." Billings grinned, tugging at Cole's sleeve. "Now let's go on down to the clubhouse, okay, Jimbo?"

He shuffled through a long, cheerless hallway,

passing people dressed like himself in ill-fitting clothes, their expressions slack and incurious. At the end of the corridor a door yawned open onto a bright dayroom.

"Here you go, Jimbo," Billings said, ushering Cole inside.

Light poured through grilled windows onto the linoleum floor. A dozen men and women in basic Kmart castoffs and ratty bathrobes milled about, staring blankly out the windows or watching the raucous cartoons blaring from a wall-mounted television. In a corner a woman desultorily pushed puzzle pieces around on a table. But Cole saw only the light—brilliant sunlight streaming through the windows like golden syrup.

"Hey, Goines!" Billings beckoned to a young man in a plaid shirt pacing in front of a window. "Yo, Jeffrey, come here—"

The man named Jeffrey Goines bounded across the room. Billings clapped a hand on Cole's shoulder and said, "Goines, this here is James. Whyncha show him around? Tell him the TV rules, show him the games and stuff, okay?"

Goines rocked back and forth on his heels. "How much you gonna pay me, huh? I'd be doing your job."

Billings grinned. "Five thousand dollars, my man. That enough? I'll wire it to your account as usual, okay?"

Goines bit his lip thoughtfully. "Okay, Billings. Five thousand. That's enough. Five thousand dollars. I'll give him the Deluxe Mental Hospital Tour."

Billings walked away, chuckling. Jeffrey turned to Cole and said conspiratorially, "Kid around, kid around. It makes them feel good, we're all pals. We're prisoners, they're the guards, but it's all in good fun, you see?"

Cole stared at this odd young man, nonplussed. Goines was young, dark-haired and blue-eyed, and as restive as a golden retriever. Compared with all those slack-jawed, empty-eyed patients staring vacantly at the TV, he looked like a preppy young intern, except for a certain furtiveness about his deepset eyes.

"C'mon," Jeffrey said. Cole nodded and followed him to the tables set beside the windows. "Here's the games," Jeffrey announced disdainfully, flicking at the edge of a Monopoly set. "Games vegetize you. If you play the games, you're voluntarily taking a tranquil-izer."

Cole said nothing, turning his head to stare down at a partially completed jigsaw puzzle showing a lion, sheep, birds, and bored-looking wolves all huddled together beneath some trees. A woman orderly patiently helped a man with trembling hands put two pieces together. THE PEACEABLE KINGDOM, the puzzle box read.

"I guess they gave you some 'chemical restraints,' huh?" Jeffrey asked, darting a glance at him. "What'd they give you? Thorazine? Haldol?" Cole stared at him blankly. "No? How about meprobamate? How much? Learn your drugs, know your doses."

"I need to make a telephone call."

Jeffrey gave a barking laugh. "A telephone call? That's communication with the outside world!

Doctor's discretion. Hey, if all these nuts could just make phone calls, it could spread! Insanity oozing through telephone cables, oozing into the ears of all those poor sane people, infecting them! Wackos everywhere! A plague of madness."

Abruptly, Jeffrey lowered his voice. "In fact, very few of us here are actually mentally ill," he whispered slyly, leaning in close to Cole's face. "I mean, I'm not saying you're not mentally ill—for all I know you're as crazy as a loon. But that's not why you're here. Why you're here is because of the system." He gestured at the television. "There's the TV. It's all right there. Commercials. We are not productive anymore; they don't need us to make things anymore; it's all automated. What are we for, then?"

Jeffrey Goines drew back, gazing at Cole expectantly. When Cole said nothing, he stabbed a finger in the air.

"We're consumers!" Jeffrey cried triumphantly. "Okay, buy a lot of stuff, you're a good citizen. But if you don't buy a lot of stuff, you know what? You're mentally ill! That's a fact! If you don't buy things— toilet paper, new cars, computerized blenders, electrically operated sexual devices—"

His voice grew more shrill, almost hysterical. "— SCREWDRIVERS WITH MINIATURE BUILT-IN RADAR DEVICES, STEREO SYSTEMS WITH BRAIN-IMPLANTED HEADPHONES, VOICE-ACTIVATED COMPUTERS—"

"Jeffrey." The orderly at the puzzle table looked up and shook her head. "Take it easy, Jeffrey. Be calm."

Jeffrey's mouth snapped shut. He closed his eyes

for a moment, took a deep breath, then continued in an utterly tranquil voice.

"So if you want to watch a particular program," he said, oblivious to the fact that Cole was staring, mesmerized, at the television, "say, *All My Children* or something, you go to the charge nurse and tell her what day and time the show you want to see is on. But you have to tell her before the show is scheduled to be on. There was this one guy who was always requesting shows that had ALREADY PLAYED!"

Cole jumped, startled, as Jeffrey began picking up speed again.

"He couldn't quite GRASP THE IDEA THAT THE CHARGE NURSE COULDN'T JUST MAKE IT BE YESTERDAY—*TURN BACK TIME!* HE WAS NUTS! A FRUITCAKE—"

"Okay, that's it, Jeffrey," the orderly said, exasperated. "You're gonna get a shot. I warned you—"

Miraculously, Jeffrey calmed himself, smiling benignly at the woman and nodding. "Right! Right!" He laughed merrily. "I got 'carried away'! Explaining the workings of . . . the institution."

Cole stared at him, amazed at Goines' transformation. Just then someone tapped him on the shoulder. Cole turned to see a somber-looking black man impeccably dressed in a dark suit, white shirt, and elegantly subdued tie.

"I don't really come from outer space," the man said by way of introduction.

Jeffrey gave Cole a sly glance. "This is L. J. Washington, Jim. He doesn't really come from outer space."

L. J. Washington shot Goines a wounded look. "Don't mock me, my friend," he said, then went on to Cole. "It's a condition called 'mental divergence.' I find myself on the planet Ogo, part of an intellectual elite, preparing to subjugate barbarian hordes on Pluto. But even though it's a totally convincing reality in every way—I can feel, breathe, hear—nevertheless, Ogo is actually a construct of my psyche. I am mentally divergent in that I am escaping certain unnamed realities that plague my life here. When I stop going there, I will be well."

Cole stared at the man's dignified face, the carefully knotted tie about his neck, and his neat faux-alligator belt. Then, glancing down for the first time, Cole saw that L. J. Washington was wearing an immense pair of fuzzy orange bedroom slippers.

"And you, my friend?" Once more the black man touched Cole gently on the shoulder, gazing with intense concern into Cole's eyes. "Are you, too, perhaps, divergent?"

Before he could reply, the muscular figure of Billings loomed up behind them. "Okay, Jimbo—conference time." The orderly clapped a huge hand on Cole's shoulder and directed him to the door. "Say good-bye to your pals. We'll see 'em again in a little while. . . . "

"Conference?" Cole wondered, glancing back over his shoulder at L. J. Washington.

"That's right. Psychiatric evaluation—pretty standard stuff, nothing to worry about," Billings added soothingly. "Right this way . . . . "

Cole walked with him, his head aching. His mouth

was parched; the acrid taste was stronger now, and he knew it must have something to do with the drugs they'd given him the night before. As he padded down the dim hallway, voices wafted out from behind closed doors: wails and laughter, a nervous giggle. He passed a room where eyes glittered from the darkness of a raised bunk and someone whispered words he couldn't understand. Cole blinked, the throbbing behind his eyes almost blinding him, and stared at his feet slapping against the linoleum in their flimsy cloth sneakers.

"Here we go—"

He was brought up short by Billings yanking at his arm. "This way, Jimbo. Doctor's waiting."

A metal door swung open, revealing a long, brightly lit room. In the middle, four men and women sat around a beat-up conference table littered with coffee mugs and manila folders. On the walls hung newspaper clippings, a schedule of recreational events, and a newsletter from Tulane Medical School. A bulletin board was plastered with notices advertising various meetings: ONE DAY AT A TIME! JUST TWELVE STEPS TO A NEW LIFE!

"Here he is, Dr. Fletcher," Billings announced. "James Cole."

The man sitting at the head of the table nodded at the orderly. Even inside, he wore tinted glasses, so that his gaze was inscrutable. "Thank you. Now, Mr. Cole—" he gestured at an empty chair "—please, have a seat."

Cole remained standing as Dr. Fletcher went on. "I'll introduce you to my colleagues: Dr. Goodin, Dr. Casey, I think you already know Dr. Railly. . . . "

For a moment Cole's eyes met Dr. Railly's. Her expression was cool, almost icily professional, but her eyes held a glint of warmth. He shook his head agitatedly. "This is a place for crazy people! I'm not crazy!"

Dr. Casey frowned slightly. "We don't use that term—'crazy'—Mr. Cole."

Cole's voice rose. Behind him Billings crossed his arms and watched him knowingly. "You've got some real nuts in here! Listen to me, all of you! I know things you don't. It's going to be difficult for you to understand, but—"

"Mr. Cole," broke in Dr. Fletcher. "Last night you told Dr. Railly you thought it was . . . "

He took a pencil from a small pile of writing implements and glanced at a file by his elbow. ". . . 1996." His gaze flicked back to Cole. "How about right now? Do you know what year it is right now?"

"1990," snapped Cole, gazing down at the conference table. "Look, I'm not confused. There's been a mistake, I've been sent to the wrong place—"

He lunged, grabbing for Dr. Fletcher's pencil. Just as his fingers closed around it, Billings' huge hand enfolded Cole's.

"Hey!" Cole cried. He looked up into Billings' implacable face—no help there—then twisted and gazed imploringly at Dr. Railly. "Tell him—I'm not going to hurt anybody."

"James, please." Kathryn Railly turned in her chair to face him. "These are all doctors here—we want to help you."

Beside her Owen Fletcher nodded. He adjusted his

tinted glasses, looked down at the pencil in Cole's fingers, and motioned at Billings. The orderly let go of Cole's wrist. Cole quickly reached for a pad of paper and began drawing.

"Do any of you know anything about the Army of the Twelve Monkeys?" Cole held up the paper, now scrawled with the crude image of a dancing monkey. "They paint this, stencil it, on buildings all over the place." He waved the paper excitedly, turning and holding it up so that first one doctor and then another could see it.

"Mr. Cole . . . " Dr. Casey murmured, shaking his head.

"Right." Cole stared at the paper dejectedly, crumpled it, and dropped it onto the floor. "I guess you wouldn't. This is only 1990, they're probably not active yet. That makes sense!" Billings eyed him watchfully as Cole began pacing the room.

"Okay—listen to me. Five billion people died in 1996 and 1997. *Five billion.*" Cole ran a hand over his stubbled scalp, then stabbed at the air with a finger. "Got that? Almost the whole population of the world! Only about one percent of us survived."

He paused, saw the doctors exchange knowing looks.

"Are you going to save us, Mr. Cole?" Dr. Goodin asked.

Cole clenched his hands in frustration. "Save you! How can I save you? It already happened! I can't save you! Nobody can! I'm simply trying to get some information to help people in the present so that they can—"

"The present?" Dr. Casey interrupted gently. "We're not in the present now, Mr. Cole?"

"No, no, this is the past." Cole's voice broke as he said with exasperated patience, "This has already happened. Listen——"

Dr. Goodin raised an eyebrow. "Mr. Cole, you believe 1996 is the 'present' then, is that it?"

"No, 1996 is the past, too. Look . . . " Cole stopped and stared at each of them in turn. In their eyes he saw nothing but cool detachment and, perhaps, pity.

"You don't believe me," he said at last. Above the bruises on his face, his cheeks reddened. "You think I'm crazy, but I'm not crazy. I'm a convict, sure, I have a quick temper, but I'm as sane as anyone in this room. I . . . "

Tap. A small sound disoriented him. *Tap, tap, tap.*

Cole looked around, feeling a faint prickling on his neck, a growing sense of unease.

Tap, tap . . .

That noise, where had he heard that—?

"Can you tell us the name of the prison you've come from?" Kathryn Railly asked softly.

Tap. Cole felt sweat breaking out on his face and chest. *Tap, tap.* He glanced down, glimpsed cold eyes behind the tinted lenses, a pencil twitching in Fletcher's hand. *Tap.*

The pencil. Memory flooded him. The microbiologist at the camp—he wore glasses like those, didn't he? Or had that been another doctor? a policeman? His icy voice had demanded, *Why did you volunteer?*

Tap.

"Does this bother you, Mr. Cole?"

Cole jumped as Dr. Fletcher's voice boomed out. The doctor held up a yellow pencil between two long thin white fingers. "It's just a pencil," said Fletcher. He smiled disarmingly. "Nervous habit of mine, that's all. . . ."

Cole shook his head, forcing the image of that other man, that other room, from his thoughts. "No!" He took a deep breath, willing himself to stay calm. "Look, I just don't belong here, okay? What I need to do is make a telephone call to straighten everything out."

Fletcher nodded, infinitely patient. "Who would you call, Mr. Cole, to straighten everything out?"

"Scientists. They'll want to know they sent me to the wrong time. I can leave a message for them, on voice mail. They monitor it from the present."

Fletcher tipped his head. "These scientists, Mr. Cole. Are they doctors like ourselves?"

Murmurs as the other psychiatrists glanced at one another.

"No!" Cole exclaimed, confused. "I mean, yes. . . . Please—one call!"

He looked desperately at Dr. Railly, his pleading eyes locking with hers. Without speaking, she nodded. A moment later Dr. Goodin handed a telephone to Cole. Cole punched the numbers in and held it to his ear as the doctors watched.

Brring. Brring.

Cole swallowed, his mouth dry, as a woman's voice shrilled, "Hello?"

"Uh, yes—" He turned so that he wouldn't see the

others staring at him. "This is, uh, James Cole. I need to leave a voice mail message for, uh——"

"Whaaat? Voice mail? Is this a joke? James who?"

He stammered, "C—Cole. James Cole——"

"Never heard of you!"

Click!

He stared in dismay at the receiver in his hand. Sympathetically, Railly reached for it and hung it up as the others looked on.

"It wasn't who you expected?" she asked gently.

"It was some lady. She didn't know anything."

"Perhaps it was a wrong number . . . ?"

"No." Cole shook his head numbly. "That's the reason they chose me. I remember things."

Dr. Railly stared at him and suddenly frowned. "James, where did you grow up? Was it around here? Around Baltimore?"

"What?" Cole replied distractedly. At the table, Railly's colleagues watched her with new interest. Fletcher's eyes narrowed and the pencil quivered in his fingers: was she showing some special interest in this patient?

Kathryn Railly shook her head slowly. Her frown faded; she was still looking at Cole, but it was as though she was seeing someone else there, someone not wearing brown polyester pants and worn white sneakers and a plastic hospital ID bracelet. "I have the . . . strangest feeling I've met you before . . . a long time ago, perhaps. Were you ever——"

Tap. "Dr. Railly!" Fletcher called. His pencil danced dangerously along the table edge. "Dr.——"

"Wait!" Cole broke in excitedly. "This is only

1990!" His eyes brightened as he went on, "I'm sup-posed to be leaving messages in 1996. It's not the right number yet—that's the problem. Damn! How can I contact them?"

Fletcher stared pointedly at Dr. Railly, one eye-brow raised. Railly flushed. Recovering her compo-sure, she crossed the room to a small cabinet, unlocked it, and removed a bottle. "Here," she said, turning briskly to Cole and pouring several pills into her palm. Her tone was cool. "James, I want you to take these."

He stared at her, torn between disbelief and rage.

"Please," she said. Behind her the other doctors stood, gathering their things. "We let you make the phone call. But now, James—"

In her outstretched hand three red-and-white cap-sules glinted. Directly behind him he could hear Billings waiting impatiently.

"James," she repeated, her voice no longer gentle. "Now, I want you to trust me."

He is at the airport again. Outside the sky is leaden, threatening. Flies batter helplessly at the observation window where he stands with his parents, staring out at a plane touching down on the runway. He thinks that he has never seen anything so beautiful, the arrowed wings and sleek white body settling smoothly onto the tarmac.

"Flight 784 now boarding at Gate . . . "

His mouth is open to ask his father if that is the plane they are going to take, when suddenly behind them there is a shout. He turns to see a ponytailed man in gaudy checked pants running past. The man is glancing over his shoulder. He doesn't see the boy; when his duffel bag slams painfully into Cole's stomach, the man glances down and yells, *"Watch it!"*

Cole starts. He knows that voice—but before he can say anything he hears a woman screaming, "Nooooo!"

The ponytailed man is gone. Another man sprints around the corner—a blond man in a Hawaiian shirt, his eyes wide as he runs toward the gate. As he passes Cole he turns, so that the boy sees his face is melting: his mouth is twisted, his mustache dangling from his upper lip. Cole gasps, but then a shot thunders through the concourse and he is blinded by dazzling white light.

"Wh—?"

He sucked his breath in and blinked awake. A few feet away a flashlight hovered in the air like ball lightning, then moved slowly on. Disoriented, Cole felt for the bedclothes: sheets, smooth and clean though rumpled, not the filthy padding strewn on the floor of his underground cell. But all around him he could hear snores and soft breathing, the occasional moan—had he been taken to another part of the prison compound? Just then he heard a low voice—a woman's voice. He turned, careful not to make any noise, peering into the darkness until he made out two figures. A female nurse and another orderly, both wearing white uniforms, walked from bed to bed, pausing with the flashlight as they checked each occupant.

Not the prison, then; at least, not *that* prison. Cole watched as the flashlight bobbed slowly down one row of beds and up another, until finally the two figures left, silently closing the door behind them.

All was dark and still, save for the murmur of restless sleepers. Cole fixed his gaze on a barred window at the far end of the room. Moonlight slanted in pale rods to the floor, made an abstract pattern of stripes and squares. For a long moment Cole stared at it, then quickly glanced around at the sleeping patients. Without a sound he slipped from his bed. Walking stealthily between the others, he made his way to the window and peered out.

Overhead the moon hung, its silvery glow filtering through the leaves of a solitary oak. Beneath the tree a couple stood embracing. Moonlight glinted off the woman's dark hair and the curve of the man's arm. Cole stared, entranced, his fingertips grazing the metal grille.

"It won't work. You can't open it."

Cole whirled to see someone sitting up in the bed nearest the window. It was Jeffrey Goines.

"You think you can remove the grille but you can't," Jeffrey went on in a matter-of-fact tone. "It's welded."

Cole turned back to the grille and gave it a perfunctory tug. In the moonlight, Jeffrey's teeth shone in a grin.

"See? I toldja." He waved loftily at the darkened room around them. "And all the doors are locked, too. They're protecting the people on the outside from us. But the people outside are as crazy as us. . . . "

Jeffrey's voice droned on as Cole stared at the windowsill. A small spider crept across the peeling paint, pausing now and then as though it knew it was being watched. Cole stared at it, fascinated, his hand groping automatically for a specimen bottle at his waist.

"Shit." Jeffrey suddenly fell silent. There was a click from the room behind them. Alarmed, Cole grabbed the spider and scrambled across the floor and back into bed, throwing the covers over himself just as the door opened and an orderly peeked inside. The blade of a flashlight probed the darkness, resting for a moment upon Cole's face, his eyes closed and mouth slightly ajar as he breathed softly. In his hand he could feel the spider struggling to free itself. After a moment the flashlight clicked off. The door closed. All was silent, until Cole heard Jeffrey's hoarse whisper.

"You know what 'crazy' is?" Jeffrey went on, as though nothing had happened. "'Crazy' is 'majority rules.'"

Cole sat up in bed, barely listening as he peered into his closed fist at the spider. Jeffrey took a deep breath and intoned, "Take germs, for example."

"Germs?" Cole shot him a look, the spider scrabbling furiously at his palm.

Jeffrey nodded. "Germs," he repeated earnestly. "In the eighteenth century there was no such thing! Nobody'd ever imagined such a thing—no sane person, anyway. Then along comes this doctor—Semmelweiss, I think. He tries to convince people—other doctors, mostly—that there are these teeny tiny invisible 'bad things' called germs that get into your body and make you sick! He's trying to get doctors to wash their hands."

Jeffrey suddenly leaned forward, leering, eyes wide as he mimed astonishment. "'What is this guy?'" he said in a funny high-pitched voice. "'Crazy? Teeny tiny invisible whaddayou call 'em—germs?!'"

Jeffrey cackled. Cole glanced at him, then back at his hand, trying to figure out what to do with the spider. Jeffrey continued, oblivious.

"Cut to the twentieth century! Last week, in fact, before I got dragged into this hellhole. I order a burger in this fast-food joint. The waiter drops it on the floor. Then he picks it up, wipes it off, hands it to me—like it was all okay. . . ."

Cole nodded absently, holding his hand up to his face. Jeffrey punched angrily at the bedclothes and hissed, "'What about the germs?' I say. He goes, 'I don't believe in germs. Germs are just a plot they made up so they can sell you disinfectants and soap.'" Jeffrey gave a triumphant hoot. "Now, *he's* crazy, right?"

Suddenly Jeffrey turned and stared at Cole with huge eyes. "Hey, you believe in germs, don't you?"

Cole stared back, his hand poised before his face. As Jeffrey watched, he popped the spider into his mouth and swallowed it.

"I'm not crazy," Cole said after a moment.

Jeffrey nodded soberly. "Of course not. I never thought you were." He tilted his head toward the moonlit window. "You wanted to escape, right? That's very sane." His voice dropped to a conspiratorial whisper. "I can help you," he said, his blue eyes glowing. "You want me to, don't you? Get you out?"

Cole shook his head. "If you know how to escape, why don't you—"

Jeffrey sat up very straight. "Why don't I escape? That's what you were going to ask me, right?" He laughed, as though Cole were a child who'd said something clever. "Cause I'd be crazy to escape! I'm all taken care of, see? I've sent out word."

Cole frowned. "What's that mean?"

"It means that I've managed to contact certain underlings, evil spirits, secretaries of secretaries, and assorted minions, who will contact my father." Jeffrey's voice rose, his blue eyes boring into Cole. "When he learns I'm in this kind of place, he'll have them transfer me to one of those classy joints where they treat you properly. LIKE A GUEST! LIKE A PERSON!"

Cole looked around nervously and edged into the center of his bed.

"SHEETS!" Jeffrey shouted, heedless of the other patients waking in the room around them. "TOWELS! LIKE A BIG HOTEL WITH GREAT DRUGS FOR THE NUTCASE LUNATIC MANIAC DEVILS—"

Cole glanced around to see people sitting up in their beds. A few whimpered. Most watched Jeffrey with the same blank interest they'd shown the television in the dayroom.

"THAT'S RIGHT! WHEN MY FATHER FINDS OUT—"

With a bang the door flew open. Patients huddled

back into their beds as the night nurse and two brawny orderlies burst into the dorm.

"Okay, that's it, Jeffrey," an orderly yelled. Too late Jeffrey tried to calm himself.

"Sorry. Really sorry," he announced, taking a deep breath. "I know—got a little agitated. The thought of escaping crossed my mind and suddenly—"

The orderlies grabbed him, one to each arm, as the nurse flourished a hypodermic needle.

"—suddenly I felt like BENDING THE FUCK-ING BARS BACK, RIPPING OFF THE GOD-DAMN WINDOW FRAMES AND—EATING THEM! YES, EATING THEM! AND LEAPING, LEAPING—"

Cole watched, fascinated and horrified, as the nurse administered the medication and the orderlies began to drag Jeffrey across the room.

"You dumb assholes!" Jeffrey shrieked, trying vainly to shake them loose. "I'm a mental patient! I'm *supposed* to act out! Wait till you morons find out who I am! My father's gonna be really upset. AND WHEN MY FATHER GETS UPSET, THE GROUND SHAKES! MY FATHER IS GOD! I WORSHIP MY FATHER!"

The door slammed shut as they hauled him into the corridor. For several minutes Jeffrey's shrill voice echoed back into the dorm, then, at last, there was silence. Cole swallowed and looked around, his heart pounding.

The room was utterly still. In the window the moon hung, crisscrossed by bars of black and gray. From the other beds came the sounds of soft breathing, mumbled nonsense words as once more the patients slept, undisturbed. Only in one bed near the window someone still sat upright, his dark eyes staring with pity at the dorm's locked door.

"You see, he, too, is mentally divergent," L. J. Washington said, turning to gaze at Cole. "But he does not accept it." He raised one hand and gestured gracefully at Cole, as though delivering a benediction, and added, "It is a better thing if you accept it, my friend. A far, far better thing." And with a peaceful smile, L. J. Washington lay back upon the bed and went to sleep.

The next morning Cole ate with the other patients in the psychiatric wing's common dining room, cold scrambled eggs and damp toast supervised by the cool gaze of Billings and another orderly. A nurse came around, administering meds. When she reached Cole she glanced down at her clipboard, frowning, then went on to the woman next to him. The nurse left; another patient nudged him and pointed to where they were to take their breakfast trays. Cole followed him, then under Billings' careful scrutiny made his way with the other patients to the dayroom.

The television was already on, tuned to a morning talk show. Dull-eyed patients slouched in cheap plastic chairs and the frayed couch, staring blankly at the TV. Cole wondered if anyone would even notice if he turned it off. He yawned, scratching idly at his sleeve. When he'd gotten up this morning, he'd found that the tiny dresser beside his bed had been outfitted with several flannel shirts and worn polyester pants. The shirts were too tight and chafed at his chest and arms, but when he'd mentioned this to Billings, the orderly had only shrugged and said, "Hey man, this ain't The Gap. Just get dressed, okay?"

Cole tugged at the collar of his shirt, wincing, then found an empty seat by a table strewn with magazines and coloring books, and a plastic bucket holding crayons and magic markers.

"Good morning," a sonorous voice pronounced.

Cole looked up and nodded at L. J. Washington. "Morning."

I wonder where he gets his clothes, he thought as Washington padded by, resplendent in three-piece suit and fuzzy bedroom slippers. Cole sank into his chair as more patients filed into the room. Except for Washington, none of them paid him the slightest bit of attention. For a few minutes he sat watching them, then began sifting through the pile of magazines. Pages were torn from all of them. In some, pictures had been defaced with obscenities or crudely drawn figures of men and women. Cole finally settled on a year-old issue of *Women's World*: it had wide margins, and only a few pages were missing. He groped among the basket of dried-out markers and pencil nubbins until he found a purple crayon long enough for him to hold comfortably. Balancing the magazine on his knee, he began writing furiously in its margins, turning the magazine upside down and sideways when he ran out of room.

He worked like that for an hour, undisturbed. In the room around him people sat quietly, the near silence broken only by the door opening to let in another patient and L. J. Washington's dignified greeting.

"Good morning, Sandra. Good morning, Dwight."

Every now and then Cole glanced up at the television. The segment on Frisbee-catching dogs had ended. Now the screen showed the gritty videotaped image of an animal, a lab monkey with shaved head, its limp body heavily restrained and so covered with wires it was difficult to make out the pallid brown form. As a narrator intoned, the monkey convulsed pathetically, its eyes wide and terrified, yellow teeth bared. Cole grimaced. He glanced around to see how the others were reacting to this disturbing image: not at all. He went back to writing in his magazine.

"Torture! Experiments!" A voice shattered the dayroom's drugged calm. Cole covered his magazine and looked up to see Jeffrey striding across the room. "We're all monkeys!"

With a small bow, Jeffrey grabbed a plastic chair and pulled it over beside Cole. "Your servant, sir," he announced with mock politesse.

Cole stared at him in dismay. "Your eye," he said, pointing at Jeffrey's face. The skin around one eye bloomed purple and livid green. "They hurt you!"

Jeffrey grinned, cocking a thumb at the television. "Not as bad as what they're doing to that kitty."

Cole turned. On TV, more taped footage showed a laboratory cat running in mad circles, eating its own tail while lab workers watched impassively. The cat's entire body was shaved bare of fur. Droplets of blood flew from its tail as it clawed in anguish at the raw flesh.

"These dramatic videotapes, secretly obtained by animal rights activists, have aroused public concern," a news reporter intoned in a voice-over. *"But authorities say there is little they can do if . . . "*

"Look at them!" Cole exclaimed angrily. "They're asking for it! Maybe people deserve to be wiped out!"

Jeffrey laughed and leaned back in his chair; he might have been happily watching a set at Wimbledon. "Wiping out the human race! That's a great idea! But it's more of a long-term thing—right now we have to focus on more immediate goals." His voice dropped to a whisper, and he reached to touch Cole's wrist reassuringly. "I didn't say a word about you-know-what."

Cole stared at him blankly. "What are you talking about?"

Jeffrey winked. "You know. Your plan. Emancipation!" He glanced down and for the first time noticed Cole's magazine. "What're you writing? You a reporter?"

"It's private." Cole shoved the magazine under one arm.

"A lawsuit? You going to sue them?" Jeffrey's eyes shone with excitement.

A shadow fell across the table. Billings loomed up beside Cole, holding out a tiny white plastic cup full of pills.

"Yo, James—time to take your meds."

"No." Cole shook his head.

"Doctor's orders." Billings produced another cup—

plastic, everything here was plastic—this one full of water, and handed it to Cole. "Come on now, Jimbo. This'll help you feel better."

Cole sat rigidly and stared at the pills. "What are they?"

Billings shrugged. "Not my job to know that, Jimbo. Drink up—"

He swallowed them. Jeffrey watched, his face expressionless.

"Now you boys be good," Billings said, crumpling the plastic cups and turning away. "Play nice."

"Sure, sure," Jeffrey said, laughing. "Real nice."

For the next few minutes Cole clutched his magazine under his arm, waiting impatiently for Jeffrey to leave. But then, slowly, his sense of urgency faded. He yawned, felt the magazine slide to the floor beside him. He left it there, and after a moment dropped the crayon as well. A bitter taste welled up in the back of his throat, but it no longer bothered him. He found himself yawning repeatedly, although he didn't feel particularly sleepy. That didn't bother him, either. After a while he must have dozed; when he opened his eyes, the TV was showing brightly lit scenes of a beautiful young couple romping ecstatically in the surf.

"*Take a chance,*" a voice urged him. "*Live the moment. Beautiful sunshine . . .* "

Nodding and yawning, Cole stood. He dragged his chair closer to the television, settling between two women staring slack-jawed at the screen.

"*. . . gorgeous beaches. Live the dream. The Florida Keys!*"

Abruptly the scene cut from the frolicking couple to a still image of the Marx Brothers. A different voice announced, "We'll return to *Monkey Business* right after these messages."

"Hey! That's pretty good." Jeffrey sidled up behind Cole, nudging him as he slid into the chair next to him. "Monkey Business. Monk Key Business."

Cole turned, bemused, as Jeffrey winked and grinned. "Get it, Jimbo? Monk—*Key*. Monk—*KEY!*"

Jeffrey held his fist out to Cole and flashed it open so that for one quick moment Cole glimpsed what it held: a key.

"Huh?" Cole shook his head groggily, then looked back up at the television, where an enormous bear moved purposely through a redwood forest.

"If you see a bearish future," a narrator droned, *"consider the changes sweeping the world . . ."*

Cole stared at the screen and nodded obediently.

"Wooo, they really dosed you up, bro," Jeffrey said, whistling. "Major load! But listen up—try and get it together! Focus! Focus!"

". . . and once you have considered, think of the opportunities they offer you . . ."

Cole turned his bleary gaze back on Jeffrey. "The *plan*," Jeffrey whispered, aggrieved. "Remember? I did *my* part!"

"What?"

"Not *what*, babe—*when!*"

Cole blinked. "When?"

With a glance over his shoulder, Jeffrey pressed the key into Cole's hand. "Now!"

Cole shook his head. "I don't—"

"But *remember*," the TV said warningly, *"to invest wisely, you need a partner . . ."*

"YES!" shrieked Jeffrey, leaping to his feet. "NOW! BUY NOW! STOCKS AND BONDS! NO MORE MONKEY BUSINESS! BUY *NOW!*"

Cole watched dumbfounded as Jeffrey danced crazily in front of him, hands flailing madly, his hair falling across his face.

"YES!" Jeffrey sang. "YES YES YES! ENHANCE YOUR PORTFOLIO *NOW!*"

Voices on the other side of the room: Cole looked over and saw Billings heading toward Jeffrey, his brooding face angry. Behind him another orderly punched numbers into a beeper.

"BUY! SELL! *SEIZE THE OPPORTUNITY!*" cried Jeffrey, his blue eyes blazing as he pirouetted in front of Cole. "ACT NOW! *DON"T DELAY!*" He danced over to where the same dull-eyed woman was laboriously moving puzzle pieces across a card table. "THIS CHANCE WON'T COME AGAIN!" With a gleeful laugh Jeffrey swept his hand across the table, sending the puzzle flying into a thousand bits. The woman gazed at the floor in disbelief, then raised her stricken face to Jeffrey. Blissfully he spun away. As Billings lunged for him, Jeffrey grabbed another patient and shoved him at the orderly.

"DON'T MISS THIS ONCE-IN-A-LIFETIME OFFER. . ."

"I'm getting dizzy!" a heavyset woman wailed as Jeffrey leaped past. "Make him *stop.*"

"Five hundred dollars!" an old man shouted suddenly into Cole's ear. "I got five hundred dollars! I'm *insured*!"

Jeffrey paused. "OPPORTUNITY!" he crowed, gazing directly at Cole. "DEFINITELY! A *WINDOW* OF OPPORTUNITY! *OPENING* NOW! NOW IS THE TIME FOR ALL GOOD MEN TO *SEIZE THE MOMENT!*"

Cole shook his head. The taste in the back of his throat was enough to make him gag. Jeffrey's words were like some thick syrup dripping slowly into his consciousness. It wasn't until he heard the dayroom door open and saw two more burly orderlies come running in after Jeffrey that it finally struck him that Jeffrey was *sending him a message*.

"YES! YES! MASTERCARD! VISA! THE *KEY* TO HAPPINESS!"

One of the orderlies paused, brandishing a hefty key ring, and quickly locked the door before turning his attention to the raving patient.

"SEIZE THE MOMENT!" Jeffrey shrieked, bounding past Billings and the other orderly. Even from across the room, Cole could see his blue eyes glowing madly as Jeffrey waved his hands. "GET RICH! NOW'S THE TIME! *GO FOR IT!*"

"Go for it," Cole repeated. He looked down at the key in his hand and looked up in time to see Billings tripping over a chair as he tried to tackle Jeffrey.

"God damn you, Jeffrey, quit playing the fool!" Billings panted.

Cole hesitated. He glanced at the door, trying to get his eyes to focus. His hand tightened on the key in his palm as the orderlies finally grabbed Jeffrey and brought him crashing to the floor.

"LAST CHANCE! LAST CHANCE! Hey—*ow!*"

Before he had a chance to think better of it, Cole staggered to the door. Feebly he stabbed at it with the key, trying vainly to find the hole. He glanced nervously over his shoulder to where the orderlies were swarming over Jeffrey. Suddenly the key slid in.

"Damn," he whispered thickly: it wouldn't turn.

"Hey."

Cole jumped, turned to see an elderly man in flannel pajamas watching him with pale watery eyes. "Florida, now *that* would be the place to go," the man said dreamily. "The Keys are lovely this time of year."

Unnerved, Cole desperately tried the key again.

It turned.

"Be careful," the old man said as Cole slipped through the door and into the echoing hallway. "J. Edgar Hoover isn't *really* dead."

Elsewhere in the county hospital, Kathryn Railly headed to her office. As she walked she riffled through the morning's stack of messages: pharmaceutical updates, urgent messages from parents and spouses inquiring after patients, notice of a change in health club hours for members. As she rounded a corner, Dr. Casey's head popped out of his office, waving a page torn from a magazine.

"Kathryn! Hang on—" She paused as Casey strode up beside her. "This was in my box, but I have a slight suspicion it wasn't meant for me."

Kathryn looked at the ragged magazine page in his hand, frowning as he began to read with exaggerated emphasis.

"You are the most beetifool woman I have ever sin. You live in a beetifool worl. But you don't know it. You have freedom, sunshine, air you can breeeth."

Her pale eyes narrowed and she gave him a sad smile. "Cole. James Cole, right?"

Casey held out a hand to silence her, adjusting his glasses as he continued, "I wood do anything to stay her, but I must leave. Pleese, help me."

Kathryn's smile faded. "Poor man . . ."

Thudding footsteps made them both turn in time to see Dr. Goodin racing around the corner.

"Hey, Kathryn!" he shouted, panting. "James Cole is one of yours, right? Well, he eloped! Last seen, he was up on nine!"

Kathryn and Casey stared, dumbfounded, then took off after him.

A security guard cornered Cole near Radiology, where he was backing out of the CAT-scan chamber. It took three guards and four orderlies to subdue him, but not without a fight. By the time they got Cole strapped to a gurney, additional security had to be called, and an ambulance.

"Please . . . you got to understand, it's a mistake, okay?" he pleaded.

"Shut up," ordered Billings.

Kathryn drew her breath in sharply when she saw them wheeling the gurney toward the isolation room.

Billings' right eye was badly swollen, and one of the security guards dabbed blood from a nasty gash on his cheek. On the gurney Cole struggled in vain with the restraints. His face was flushed and blotchy, his pupils dilated. She was stunned by how much urgency he could still pump into his slurred words—he'd had enough Halcion to trank out someone twice his size.

"Dr. Railly?" Billings' voice broke her reverie. She moved aside to let them wheel Cole into the room.

"Yes," she replied. She tapped the hypo, checking once more for air bubbles, then turned to Cole. He stared at her with wide mad eyes, and she thought back to a night last summer, when she'd accidentally run over a raccoon. It had looked at her like that, scarcely comprehending and numb with pain, its teeth bared in a bloody grimace.

"No more drugs. Please . . ." Cole whispered.

Railly swallowed, forcing herself to stare at his hand and not his eyes. "It's just something to calm you," she said as she pressed the needle against the skin of his upper arm. "I have to do this, James. You're very confused."

Before one of the guards could question her, she turned and fled, trying not to remember how, a year before, she had heard the raccoon snarling and thrashing at the side of the road as she drove away.

She made her rounds, then returned to her office. On her desk was a message for her to meet with Dr. Fletcher in the conference room.

"Shit," she murmured, rubbing her throbbing temples. She gulped down several ibuprofen, chasing them with a mouthful of tepid Evian water, and hurried back into the hall.

In the conference room, Dr. Fletcher sat between Goodin and Casey. All three looked tense, Goodin bordering on outright anger. Kathryn felt herself grow hot, flashing back to high school visits to the principal's office.

"Kathryn, sit down."

Fletcher waved at the chair across from him. Kathryn glanced at it, then quickly moved another chair to the table and sat in it. Fletcher's eye twitched as he reached for his pencil and exclaimed, "Four years! We've worked together for *four years*, Kathryn, I've never seen you like this before."

Kathryn opened her mouth and Fletcher pointed his pencil at her. "Now please, Kathryn, stop being so defensive. This isn't an inquisition."

"I didn't think I was being defensive. I was just—"

The pencil came down, hard, on the edge of the conference table. *"He should have been in restraints. It was bad judgment on your part, plain and simple. Why not just cop to it?"*

Kathryn started to snap back, then thought better of it. Instead she stared at the table for a long moment.

"Okay, it was bad judgment," she said at last. An unwanted vision rose before her: Cole's helpless form strapped to the gurney with canvas-and-metal bonds. "But I have the strangest feeling about him, I've seen him somewhere and—"

"He's already put two policemen in the hospital," Fletcher interrupted angrily. "And now we have an orderly with a broken arm and a security officer with a fractured skull!"

"I said it was bad judgment! What else do you want me to say?"

Fletcher leaned back in his chair. "You see what I mean? You're being defensive." He turned to Dr. Casey. "Isn't she being defensive, Bob?"

Before Casey could reply, there was a tentative knock at the door. Kathryn swung around and saw Billings holding an ice pack to his face as he said, "Uh, Dr. Fletcher? We got another—situation."

"*Christ,*" Fletcher swore, slamming his hand against the table. This time the pencil snapped in two. "*Now* what is it?"

Billings pulled the ice pack away from his cheek and winced. "I think you better see for yourself, Doctor."

They filed into the hall behind Fletcher, Billings studiously avoiding Kathryn's eyes as he led them toward isolation.

In front of the entrance to the padded cell a small crowd was gathered, several security guards and a day nurse. Fletcher bulled his way through them, shoved the heavy door open and stared inside.

"Where is he?"

Behind him Billings shook his head. "He's—he's gone, Doctor."

"He was in full restraints?" Fletcher's voice rose dangerously. Kathryn braced herself for what was coming. "And the door was locked?"

Billings nodded. "Yes, sir. Did it myself."

"And he was fully sedated?"

Kathryn met his accusing gaze and replied, "He was *fully* sedated!"

Fletcher pounded the door's padded interior. "Are you trying to tell me," he exploded, "that a *fully* sedated, *fully* restrained patient somehow slipped out a vent, replaced the grille behind him, and that he's wriggling through the ventilation system *right now?*"

All eyes fixed on what Fletcher was pointing at: a vent set a good eight feet from the floor and covered with a heavy stainless-steel grille. It was all of five inches square.

"Is that what you're trying to tell me?" Fletcher repeated, glaring at Billings. The orderly shrugged uneasily, his gaze still on the vent.

"Uh, yeah, Dr. Fletcher," he said as more security personnel came running down the hall to join them. "I guess that's exactly what I'm telling you."

The glass that makes up the observation window is thick and whorled with dust and grease, the smeared impressions left by a thousand other children pressing their faces against its cool surface. Outside a 747 climbs cleanly into the air, the ground shimmering in the heat of its engines.

"Flight 784 to San Francisco is now boarding at Gate Thirty-Eight. Flight 784 . . ."

Behind him are voices, the first hesitant cries of a gathering crowd. He whirls, trying to shrug off his father's hand, and sees a blond ponytailed man go barreling past. The little crowd scatters as travelers dive for cover, and for an instant he glimpses a woman standing there, her hands drawn to her mouth as she shouts.

"Nooooooo!"

He frowns. There is something familiar about her—the pale blue eyes, the determined yet graceful set of her mouth, the angle at which her head is cocked. The image of another woman comes to him. A woman with dark hair and pitying eyes, a doctor—what was her name? A doctor—

Yet the woman in the airport is very blond and heavily made up: her full mouth a gleaming slash of red, her pale skin shadowed by mascara. Her blue eyes are wide, her mouth is open but oddly unmoving as she bleats in an unearthly voice—

"The Freedom for Animals Association now boarding on Second Avenue. Secret Headquarters, Gate Sixteen. Army of the Twelve Monkeys . . ."

"Cole, you moron! Wake up!"

His eyes blinked open as the digitized monotone of a PA system continued to drone on in that same bloodless tone—

" . . . of the Twelve Monkeys. They're the ones who are going to do it."

"Cole!"

Cole sat slumped in a chair. He tried to straighten but could not, he was too weak; he could only blink again, focusing on the source of the sound: a tape recorder set on a table. Behind it was a row of scowling faces. The camp scientists, or were they doctors? He closed his eyes for a moment, fighting a wave of pain and nausea.

". . . I can't do anything more. I have to go now. Have a merry Christmas."

He opened his eyes. The voice died abruptly as the tape ran off the reel, flapping noisily in the too-still room.

"Well?" It was the earnest astrophysicist with the elegant gray hair and one gold earring.

Cole swallowed, his mouth dry and chalky. "Uh, what?" he croaked.

"He's drugged out of his mind!" one of the other scientists snapped. "He's completely zoned out."

The astrophysicist ignored him. "Cole," he asked, pointing at the tape recorder, "did you or did you not record that message?"

Cole blinked painfully, trying to get a better look at the tape recorder. "Uh, that message . . . me?"

"It's a reconstruction of a deteriorated recording," one of the other scientists explained with forced composure. "A weak signal on our number. We have to piece them together one word at a time, like jigsaw puzzles."

"We just finished rebuilding this," the astrophysicist broke in. "Did you or did you not make this call?"

Anger finally fought its way through Cole's haze. "I couldn't call! You sent me to the wrong year! It was 1990!"

"1990!"

The scientists turned to one another, whispering frantically. Then, "You're certain of that?" one asked. Before Cole could answer, the microbiologist broke in, his black spectacles glinting in the dim light.

"What did you do with your time, Cole?" he

asked in an ominous voice. "Did you waste it on drugs? Women?"

Cole said thickly, "They forced me to take drugs."

"Forced you!" The microbiologist looked at the others in disbelief. "Why would someone force you to take drugs?"

"I got into trouble." Cole spoke slowly, trying to piece it all together for himself as well as his anxious audience. "I got arrested. But I still got you a specimen, a spider. But I didn't have anyplace to put it, so I ate it. It was the wrong year anyway, so I guess it doesn't matter."

His voice trailed off. The scientists stared at him incredulously, then turned and once more began whispering among themselves. Cole struggled to keep his eyes open. The effort of speaking had left him exhausted. His head ached, and his jaw—had he been struck? He couldn't remember, didn't *want* to remember.

His head lolled forward. His vision clouded so that the face in front of him—the microbiologist—blurred, suddenly took on the sharper contours and glittering eyes of the man in the conference room. The man with the pencil: Dr. Fletcher. Cole sucked his breath in, forced himself to stare until the outlines of the man's face softened and he could see him again—not Dr. Fletcher but the microbiologist, a pencil twitching between his fingers. With a small cry Cole slumped forward, and the room went black.

He had no idea how long he slept, if indeed he slept at all. Once upon a time, Cole had believed there was a great gap between wakefulness and sleep, between life and dream-life, between what he recalled as real and what he knew to be fragments of that other, twilight world.

But now all that had changed. Like the microbiologist's face, his perceptions melted and were then reformed by whatever weird visual or auditory cues his mind picked up on. Brainwashed prisoners felt like this, and drug addicts, and schizophrenics . . .

Which was he?

"Cole!"

He woke with a start. Around him all was dark, save for where a slide was being projected on a torn screen.

"What about it, Cole?" the voice boomed. "Did you see this when you went back?"

Cole squinted. The slide showed stenciled graffiti in dull red paint, a circle enclosing twelve dancing monkeys.

"Uh, n—no, sir," Cole stammered. "I—"

Click. Another slide appeared. Protesters, young skinheads and angry women waving placards and sheets spray-painted with slogans.

MEAT = DEATH!

MILK MEANS BLOOD!

NO MORE CRUELTY!

Behind placards showing grimacing capuchin monkeys and blinded cats, policemen in riot gear confronted the crowd.

"What about these people?" The astrophysicist's voice was low. "Did you see any of these people?"

Click. A close-up of the same slide, zooming in on the much-enlarged, blurry face of a man holding a torn photo of a vivisected monkey. The man's face was as contorted as the animal's, his rage mirroring the monkey's anguish. Cole gaped at the slide in disbelief. Despite his long hair and glasses, the man resembled a slightly older Jeffrey Goines.

"Huh?" The astrophysicist tugged at his earring, urging Cole to go on. "Him? You saw that man?"

Cole nodded. "Uh, I think so. In the mental hospital."

"You were in a mental institution?" The slide disappeared in a blaze of light. Cole shielded his eyes as the microbiologist stepped in front of the screen. "You were sent to make very important observations!"

"You could have made a real contribution." The astrophysicist shook his head, disappointed. "Helped to reclaim the planet."

"As well as reducing your sentence," one of the other scientists added darkly.

"The question is, Cole," the microbiologist said, pulling up a chair beside him. *"Do you want another chance?"*

Behind him a jet engine shrieks, its wail nearly drowned by confused shouts, the sound of myriad footsteps running. When he raises his head, the boy sees the blond woman fleeing up the concourse, her bright hair flapping against her back. Someone bumps him and he opens his mouth to cry out.

"Who's that?" a raspy voice demands.

Cole blinked awake.

"I said, *who's that?*" The same voice, petulant now, almost mocking. Cole rubbed his eyes, his fingers smeared with grit, and stared blearily into the dimness. A tiny cell, with the same bare cement walls, the same high ceiling as the isolation room at the county hospital. There was no one in it but himself.

"Hey, Bob—what's your name?"

Cole dug his elbows into his pallet and raised himself, looking around in vain for the source of the voice. Was this part of the dream? He shook his head, trying to force himself into full wakefulness. His head felt numb, his mouth was raw and tasted of bile.

"Yo, Bob! Whatsamatta, cat got your—"

Suddenly Cole's eyes focused on a vent no wider than his hand, high up on the wall. Could the voice be coming from there? "Where are you?" he croaked.

The voice laughed with a nasty jubilance. "You can talk! Whaddja do, Bobby Boy? Volunteer?"

Cole squinted at the vent. "My name's not Bob," he said at last.

"No prob, Bob. Where'd they send you?"

Cole licked his lips, tasted dried blood. "Where are you?" he asked.

A pause. Then, "Another cell—maybe."

Cole winced and pulled himself upright, straining to see something behind the vent's steel mesh—a face, a shadow, a hand, anything. "What do you mean, 'maybe'? What's that supposed to mean?"

"'Maybe' means *maybe* I'm in the next cell, another

volunteer like you. Or *maybe* I'm in the central office spying on you for all those science bozos. Or, hey—"

The voice took on a more ominous tone. *"Maybe I'm not even here. Maybe I'm just in your head. No way to confirm anything, right? Ha ha. Where'd they send you?"*

Cole hunched silently on his pallet.

"Not talking, huh, Bob? That's okay. I can handle that."

"1990."

"Ninety!" the voice exclaimed in exaggerated delight. "Oooh! How was it? Good drugs? Lotsa pussy? Hey, Bob, you do the job? Didja find out the big info? Army of the Twelve Monkeys? Where the virus was prior to mutation?"

"It was supposed to be 1996."

The voice cackled. "Science isn't exactly an exact science with these clowns, but they're getting better. Hey, you're lucky you didn't end up in ancient Egypt!"

A rattle of keys in the door behind Cole. He turned, painfully, as the voice whispered, "Shhh! They're coming!"

The door creaked open and two guards stepped in, wheeling an ancient gurney. Cole let himself be strapped to it without protest. As they pushed him into the corridor, his eyes remained fixed on the vent in the wall, its steel grille a mouth drawn in a grimace.

It took them only minutes to reach their destination, a gloomy chamber lit by a single flickering fluorescent bulb. The room's walls were of cracked concrete, pleached with mildew. Veins of water bled onto the floor. Cole could hear a soft slurping as the gurney's wheels slid through puddles rank with mold.

"Well, Cole. No mistakes this time." Several pairs of gloved hands tightened the restraints. "Stay alert. Keep your eyes open."

Cole recognized the earnest tones of the silver-haired astrophysicist, but in the darkness all he saw were pale faces, a row of white-clad bodies moving efficiently through the murk.

"Good thinking about that spider, Cole." The zoologist's gentle voice sounded in his ear as the gurney creaked forward. She stroked his arm, let her hand rest for a moment on his forehead. "Try and do something like that again. Here, now—"

At the end of the room he could just make out a huge, rounded shape, an immense, faintly glowing tube made of some kind of transparent material. Cole's heart began to pound. He had seen this before, where had he seen this? In his dream, at the airport? Or, no—a flash as he momentarily saw a room at the county hospital where he had fled before Billings tackled him. A technician's stunned face, a sign on the door reading CAT SCAN AUTHORIZED PERSONNEL ONLY. As he stared at it in growing horror, the tube began to darken, like a clear glass filled with cobalt liquid.

"Just relax now. Don't fight it." The zoologist slipped away. In her place stood the microbiologist, his dark glasses glinting in the bluish light. "We have to know what's there so we can fix it."

Then he was gone, too. Above Cole there was

only the shadowy maw of the glowing tube, a blur of anxious faces. The gurney gave a last whining shriek as it was pushed into the opening. The door to the tube clanged shut.

Sudden, unexpected darkness. *True* darkness, the airless black night of a sealed casket. Cole closed his eyes, opened them: there was no difference. No flickering blue glow, not even those phantom colors that come between waking and dream. He began to move, desperately, shifting his weight from side to side so that the gurney rattled. He grunted with fear, opened his mouth to yell but then thought, *Air! There's no air!* But before he could even gasp a sound came to him—*surrounded* him—a low, mechanical hum like a swarm of electric bees. The hum grew louder, and louder still, until he could feel his bones vibrating. Lightning tore through the darkness— once, twice—resolved into a blinding strobe that pulsed in time with the deafening roar. Cole could no longer tell if he was hearing that horrific sound, or if he had been truly deafened and was merely sensing it in his battered body.

But then, miraculously, the sound diminished, so slowly that it was several moments before Cole registered that the thunder had softened to a growl, the growl to a hum, the hum to staccato crackling. His ears rang, and there was a tinny whine that somehow resolved itself into voices, though he could make out no words, only frenzied cries, a shout. As abruptly as it had begun, the strobing ceased. The restraints chafed at his arms, his chest felt as though it would burst as he strove to raise himself from the gurney. He cried out as a metal buckle pierced his flesh, his voice swallowed by a sudden explosion.

"*AAAGHHH!*"

All about him the darkness shattered, fell onto him in a rain of stones and earth. With a shout Cole fell backward, his hands flailing against something that thudded to the ground beside him. He looked up and saw gray sky. In front of him was an earthen wall studded with broken roots and bits of metal. A soft disconsolate rain pattered upon his upraised face. When he opened his mouth rain streamed inside, bringing with it the cold bite of dirt.

"*Non! C'est mon bras—!*"

Cole stared uncomprehending as first one figure shoved past him, then another. Their faces were covered with grotesque masks. Corrugated tubes fed into their mouths. Unthinkingly Cole groped at his own face, but found no mask there; only grime and blood. A sudden gust sent rain sluicing into the trench. Another explosion sent a spume of earth flying across the trench's opening. There was an answering chatter of gunfire. Cole shivered and for the first time looked down.

He was naked. Shocked, he ran a hand across his chest, brought it to his face smeared with mud and what felt like a bit of wet tissue. When he spread his fingers he saw trapped between them the limp remnant of another finger. A tiny shaft of bone protruded from it, like a tooth.

"*Arrête!*"

Cole turned, frantically trying to fling the bit of savaged bone from his hand.

"*Qui est–?*"

A man in a dun-colored uniform stood in front of him, shouting. Cole stared at him open-mouthed: the archaic cut of his clothes, the filthy puttees wound around his legs. The rifle he clutched menacingly was topped with a foot-long bayonet.

"Where's your mask? And your clothes—and your *weapon*, you idiot!" the man shouted at him in French.

Cole backed away from him, teeth chattering. "What? *What?*"

"Out of the way!" the man continued.

Cole fell back into a half-crouch as several men pushed past him, carrying a stretcher piled with stones. Torn and bloody canvas hung from it in long strands. It wasn't until the stench of burnt flesh filled his nostrils that Cole realized the bloodstained canvas was actually the remains of a man's arms, the misshapen stones the crushed pulp of his skull and shattered chest.

"Oh, my God—"

"Captain!" the man shouted in French. Cole doubled over as the bayonet jabbed him in the ribs. "A Kraut! We got a Kraut!"

"I don't understand!" Cole gasped, clutching his stomach. "Where am I? Who—"

"How'd you get here, soldier?" a voice spoke in German. Another man stepped through the mud, bespectacled and smaller than the first, wearing what was undoubtedly an officer's uniform. "What's your rank? Where are your clothes?"

Cole shook his head. "I—I don't understand."

"German! Speak German! What are you doing here?"

Cole began to shake uncontrollably. His vision blurred, the background chatter of gunfire and unintelligible voices droned into a single sound, a high-pitched whining that might have been a siren or Cole's own voice. He felt giddy and nauseated, but he no longer cared; he had gone beyond fear or bewilderment or torture to some other place. His eyes were open, but he saw nothing. The sergeant jabbed him again, but it didn't hurt—how could it hurt? The edges of his consciousness were pulling away from his mind like burning paper; in a few moments there would be nothing left but a vacant-eyed man. In a trench or a cell, strapped to a gurney or stumbling through an airport lobby—how could it matter? Even that shrill whine was dying away, but Cole felt only a dull relief. He would have smiled, but even that was too much of an effort; it would only be another instant and he would be gone, gone—

"I gotta find 'em! I gotta find 'em! Please, you gotta help me!"

The voice was like a shard of glass tearing through his fugue state.

"Please!"

English, but accented English—accented *American* English. The sergeant jabbed him again and this time Cole flinched, blinking as he suddenly focused on another stretcher being borne past him.

"Please, you gotta listen, I got to—"

On the stretcher a young man thrashed. Blood

covered his face and arms and chest, dripped in a thin line from the corners of the canvas to the wet ground. In his blackened face his eyes rolled wildly. Staring at him Cole felt a horror more intense than any that had come before.

"Jose!" he screamed. It was the boy from the cell next to his. *"Jose!"*

The boy turned. "Cole!" His face contorted in anguish. "Oh God, Cole, where are we?"

His hand reached feebly for Cole's. Before Cole could grasp it, a man darted behind them. There was a flash of light, the stale scent of saltpeter as the photographer crouched in the trench, his unwieldy camera focused on Jose.

"No—" Cole cried brokenly. Without pausing the photographer clutched his camera to his chest and scurried on. Shots rang out; Cole gasped, grabbed for his left leg and fell.

Gritting his teeth he tried to push himself back up, grimacing at the pain. A whistling overhead ended in a thump that sent more dirt raining into the trench. There were muffled shouts, commands he could not understand. Down the sides of the trench coiled thick yellow smoke. A poisonous stench filled Cole's nostrils and he coughed, covering his mouth and looking around frantically. The trench grew thick with soldiers in gas masks, like ants in a disturbed nest. Coughing, Cole knelt on his good leg and covered his streaming eyes as he searched for some way out. His gaze fell on a jackknifed form beside him: the captain, his chest split as neatly as a capon's. From his face dangled a gas mask. With a cry Cole propelled himself forward, fingers snatching for the mask, but before he could grab it another explosion ripped through the trench. The last thing Cole saw was his own face, reflected in the captain's shattered glasses.

On a chill evening in late autumn, a few brown leaves still clung to the oak trees outside of Breitrose Hall. Squirrels worried at a clutch of acorns, and in the velvety sky overhead an owl flew, crying mournfully. Tacked to the building's gothic facade were flyers advertising a local band, index cards bearing urgent pleas from students for rides home for the Thanksgiving holiday, an out-of-date listing of campus movies. A handful of students crossed lazily in front of the steps, pausing beneath a streetlight to read the newest placard there:

THE ALEXANDER LECTURES, WINTER 1996

JON ELSE ON
The Nuclear Agony
DR. ALEXANDER MIKSZTAL ON
Biological Ethics
MICHELLE DEPRIEU ON
Chernobyl: Accident or Mass Psychosis?
DRS. HELEN & HOWARD STEERING ON . . .

Across the top of the placard a taped, handwritten banner read:

TODAY!! NOVEMBER 19TH
DR. KATHRYN RAILLY
Madness and Apocalyptic Visions

Inside, the lecture hall was nearly full. A woman's voice echoed hollowly through the cavernous space, punctuated every now and then by coughing, the rustle of papers. Across a giant screen in the front of the room loomed the projected image of a man's face, crudely but effectively drawn in the bold strokes of a medieval woodcut. His eyes were huge and mad, his mouth agape as though in mortal agony.

"'And one of the four beasts gave unto the seven angels seven golden vials full of the wrath of God, who liveth forever and ever.'"

The woman speaking at the podium lifted her head. Tall and fine-boned, her dark hair swept into a neat chignon, she was the epitome of academic elegance, striking yet restrained: large-framed tortoise-shell glasses, chic black suit that didn't show too much leg, only a faint hint of color in her porcelain skin. Her voice matched her, refined but powerful. She paused, giving her audience a moment to savor her words, then went on.

"Revelations. In the twelfth century, according to the accounts of local officials at that time, *this* man—"

Her pointer indicated the raving madman on the screen.

"—appeared suddenly in the village of Wylye near Stonehenge in Wiltshire, England, in April of 1162. Using unfamiliar words and speaking in a strange accent, the man made dire prognostications about a pestilence which he predicted would wipe out humanity in approximately eight hundred years."

The slide changed to one showing the ruins of Stonehenge, bathed in moonlight that gave them a troubling glow. More rustlings from the audience, this time punctuated with a few impatient huffs.

"Dr. Railly," a voice at the back of the room began chidingly, but the woman at the podium continued without a beat.

"Deranged and hysterical," she pronounced, "the man raped a young woman of the village, was taken into custody, but then mysteriously escaped and was not heard of again. Now—"

She looked into the darkened lecture hall, the pool of light on her face making her look like a somber angel. "Obviously, this plague/doomsday scenario is considerably more compelling when reality supports it with a virulent disease, whether it's the bubonic plague, smallpox, or AIDS. And now we have technological horrors as well, such as chemical warfare, which first reared its ugly head in the deadly mustard gas attacks of World War One."

On the screen behind her, a series of slides showed images of doughboys in gas masks, an unexploded bomb, the skeletal rictus of a boy's face in the last agonies of death by gas. *"Dulce et decorum est pro patria mori,"* Railly remarked dryly. "During one such attack in the French trenches in October 1917, we have an account of *this* soldier—"

Her pointer touched the screen. A sepia-toned photograph showed a dark-haired young man, his features all but obscured by blood, being borne on a stretcher by exhausted soldiers. The man's wounded hand was outstretched, his expression almost unbearably poignant, the face of someone who has found his heart's desire only to have it snatched from his grasp.

"During an assault, he was wounded by shrapnel and hospitalized, apparently in a state of hysteria. Doctors found he had lost all comprehension of French. But he spoke English fluently, albeit in a regional dialect they didn't recognize. The man, although physically unaffected by the gas, was hysterical. He claimed he had come from the future, that he was looking for a pure germ that would ultimately wipe mankind off the face of the earth, starting in the year—1996!"

Nervous chuckles from the audience. Railly tapped the screen impatiently as another photograph came into focus. This one revealed the gaunt, haunted image of the same young man, staring with ravaged eyes from the narrow cot of a military hospital.

"Though injured, the young soldier disappeared from the hospital, no doubt trying to carry on his mission to warn others, substituting for the universally acknowledged agony of war a self-inflicted agony we call 'the Cassandra Complex.'"

In the hall, two listeners nodded raptly, then glanced smiling at each other—Marilou Martin and Wayne Chang, friends of Railly's from her university days. A few seats away from them, someone else was having a harder time buying Railly's theory.

"Doodling while Rome burns," a man muttered darkly. Marilou turned, frowning, and saw a black-clad man with shoulder-length red hair tapping ferociously at a laptop computer in between glares at Dr. Railly.

"As you recall," Railly went on somewhat breathlessly, "in Greek legend Cassandra was condemned to *know* the future, but to be *disbelieved* when she told it. Hence the agony of foreknowledge combined with impotence to do anything about it."

The lecture continued in this vein for another hour. At last, a final image filled the screen: the face of the raving madman from the woodcut, superimposed with that of the haunted soldier and the rabid face of the lead singer of an alternative band popular for its doomy lyrics.

"Thank you," Railly said, suddenly shy. She ducked her head and turned from the podium, then hurried from the lecture hall.

In a reception room on the second floor of Breitrose, members of the university's psych department had set up a table with dip and raw vegetables and a few tired-looking cold cuts. Railly grabbed a carrot and a glass of seltzer and settled at a library table at the front of the room. Stacks of books bore identical dust jackets in ominous shades of orange and crimson, overlaid with the same black-and-white medieval engraving of a wild-faced man.

THE DOOMSDAY SYNDROME:
APOCALYPTIC VISIONS OF THE MENTALLY ILL
BY DR. KATHRYN RAILLY

Moments later, the first enthusiastic members of the audience began drifting through the door. A few wan souls congregated around the crudités, but most made a beeline for Railly, lofting copies of the book and thrusting them into her face.

"What a wonderful meditation on such a complex topic," a tweedy woman began, when she was pushed aside by a lanky red-haired man in black.

"Dr. Railly," he proclaimed loudly. DR. PETERS was scrawled on his name tag in black Magic Marker. His voice scraped rawly through the others as he announced, "*I* think you have given your 'alarmists' a bad name. Surely there is very *real* and very *convincing* data that the *planet* cannot *survive* the excesses of the human race: proliferation of atomic devices, uncontrolled breeding habits, the rape of the environment, the pollution of land, sea, and air."

He paused for breath, and people began to edge back toward the cold cuts. A few hardy grad students remained to listen, nodding or shaking their heads as the man went on.

"In *this* context, isn't it obvious that 'Chicken Little' represents the *sane* vision, and Homo sapiens' motto, '*Let's Go Shopping!*' is the cry of the *true* lunatic?"

Having delivered his little bombshell, Dr. Peters gave Kathryn Railly a tight, self-important smile. Before she could respond, an elderly disheveled professor elbowed past him.

"Dr. Railly! Please!" The old man thumped a tattered manuscript on the table in front of her. "I wonder if you're aware of my own studies, which indicate that certain cycles of the moon actually impact on the incidence of apocalyptic predictions as observed in urban emergency rooms—"

Kathryn shook her head helplessly. "Uh, no. Actually—"

"In fact," the professor babbled on, "birthing centers in Scandinavia have charted an alarming increase in the number of . . . "

Kathryn Railly's eyes glazed over, even as she continued to nod and murmur politely.

". . . not to mention the link between drug abuse and solar flares, which has been pointedly *ignored* by—"

"Kathryn—"

A hand touched her shoulder. Kathryn turned, sighing in relief when she saw Marilou and Wayne standing behind her.

"You were *great*," said Marilou. She cast a baleful glance at the reception table, where Dr. Peters was scarfing down raw cauliflower. "Really, really great."

Kathryn squeezed her hand. "You're leaving?" she asked, trying to keep disappointment from edging into her voice.

Marilou looked apologetic. "Our reservation's at nine thirty. It's getting late."

Another hand grabbed Kathryn's other shoulder. "Dr. Railly!" the elderly man cried. "Please—this is very important!"

Wayne Chang made a face. "You sure you're gonna be all right?" He cocked a thumb at the apoplectic professor.

Kathryn laughed and glanced at her watch. "You go ahead. I'll be there in twenty minutes."

"Okay." Wayne nodded, taking Marilou's arm. "We'll make sure the champagne's good and cold."

Kathryn watched her friends walk off as the professor rambled on. "Dr. Railly, I simply cannot understand your exclusion of the moon in relation to apocalyptic dementia . . . "

With a sigh, Kathryn turned back to him. "I left out wolfbane and garlic, too," she said, then tried to cover her exasperation by adding, "But I'd be happy to take a look at your paper."

The professor beamed. "Well, thank you," he said. Straightening, he stretched out a gnarly hand and picked up a copy of her book. "Perhaps then you could sign this for me? As one colleague to another?"

Kathryn smiled. "Of course," she said gently, and reached for her pen.

Half an hour later she left. Several members of the psych department escorted her outside, then waved good-bye as they headed to their own cars. Kathryn pulled her coat tight about her, wishing she'd brought a scarf. The chill early evening had turned downright cold. In little over a month it would be Christmas. Overhead a full moon gleamed, casting baroque shadows on the ornate turrets and arches of Breitrose Hall. Kathryn hurried across the parking lot to her Cherokee, one of the last cars still parked there. Her footsteps echoed loudly against the concrete, and she looked up when a Volvo roared past.

"Congratulations!" someone yelled. Kathryn waved happily as behind her the last yellow lights of Breitrose Hall went dark. A few more steps and she reached her car. She fished in her purse for the keys, hoping that Marilou and Wayne really *had* ordered champagne—she hadn't felt this exhilarated since she'd finished her thesis. She unlocked the car door, tossed her purse onto the passenger seat, and was just ducking inside when a shadow fell across her.

"Hello—?" she began tentatively.

Someone grabbed her in a choke hold, pulling her back so roughly she could only gasp.

"Get in!" a hoarse voice ordered. Kathryn writhed around to see a large man silhouetted against the moonlit sky. Unable to scream, she kicked at him, gasping for breath, as he forced her into the front seat.

"I've got a gun."

She froze. The man slammed the front door shut, then opened the rear door and scrambled in behind her. Glancing into the rearview mirror, she saw only piercing black eyes staring at her from the shadows.

"You—you can have my purse." It hurt to talk, but she tried desperately to keep the quaver from her voice. "I have a lot of cash and credit—"

"Start the car."

Half-turning in her seat, she thrust the keys at him. "Here!" she said desperately. "You can have the keys. You can—"

He lunged, grabbing her hair and yanking her head back so hard she felt the tendons pop.

"Start the car!" he repeated fiercely in her ear. "*Now!*"

A moment later the engine roared to life. She backed the car from the lot and headed for the exit, her hands shaking as they gripped the steering wheel. In the mirror she could glimpse the man's eyes flickering as they passed beneath one streetlamp after another.

"I don't want to hurt you," he said softly, his voice more calm now. "But I will. I've hurt people before, when—*left! Turn left!*"

She yanked the wheel left, hunching forward and praying he wouldn't grab her again. When she glanced back, she saw him unfolding a tattered map. His face was lost in darkness, but now and then she had a glimpse of ragged clothing as he tried to read the map by the intermittent glow of the street lights.

After a few minutes had passed in silence, Kathryn took a deep breath, then asked, "Where—where are we going?"

"Philadelphia," the man said tersely.

"Philadelphia!" Kathryn flashed him a quick stunned look. "But that's—that's more than a hundred miles!"

"That's why I can't walk there," the man said without a trace of irony. "Turn here—I think."

She obeyed, watching him in the mirror as he tried to read. When she looked back at the road again, her heart leapt. Gliding through the darkness was a police car. Kathryn hesitated, then with a quick glance at the mirror switched on her car's dome light.

"This will help you," she said, her voice cracking.

A fist crashed through the air, smashing the light. Splinters of plastic sprayed Kathryn's shoulders as she bit her lip, fighting tears as the police car passed. In the seat behind her, the man crouched, hiding his face until the car was gone. When he slid back upright, Kathryn spoke, heedless of her trembling voice.

"If you make me go with you, it's kidnapping. That's a serious crime. If you let me go, you could just take the car and—"

"I don't know how to drive!" the man shouted. "We went underground when I was six, I told you that. When you come to the corner, turn—"

She slammed on the brakes, whirled, and for the first time looked right at him.

"Cole! James Cole! You escaped from a locked room six years ago!"

A car pulled up behind them and honked angrily.

"1990," Cole snapped. "Six years for *you*. Come on," he added, glancing anxiously at the car behind them. "Take a right turn there."

She turned onto the access ramp for the freeway. Looking back, she saw Cole settling wearily against the seat. Dirt smudged his face; his close-cropped hair was mud-caked. Kathryn hesitated, measuring her words, then said, "I can't believe this is a coincidence, Mr. Cole. Have you been . . . *following* me?"

He lifted his head. His haggard face filled the tiny mirror. "You told me you'd help me," he said wearily. "I know this isn't what you meant, but—I'm desperate. I got no money, a bum leg. I been sleeping on the streets." He paused, wincing, and shot her an apologetic grimace. "Sorry about that."

Kathryn's heart slowed its pounding. A kind of nightmare edginess took over, equal parts despair and anger. "You *have* been following me, haven't you?"

Cole shook his head. "No. I saw this—"

He rummaged in a pocket, triumphantly held up a frayed piece of paper—the flyer for her lecture. "—in a store window." Pride swelled in his voice. "I can read, remember?"

Kathryn nudged the car through freeway traffic. "Yes. I remember." She bit her lip, then asked, "Why do you want to go to Philadelphia?"

Cole reached for her purse, dragged it into the backseat beside him and started sifting through its contents. "I checked out the Baltimore information; it was nothing. It's Philadelphia, that's where they are. The ones who did it—the Twelve Monkeys."

He leaned over the front seat. "You got any food? Hey!" He pointed eagerly at the dashboard. "Is that a radio?"

Kathryn switched it on. Through the speakers filtered pounding surf and keening gulls, an oozing baritone.

"This is a personal message to you. *Are you at the end of your rope? Are you dying to get away?"*

Cole stiffened, listening intently.

"The Florida Keys are waiting for you . . ."

Cole frowned as the sound of crashing surf mingled with the cries of seabirds in the car. Watching him Kathryn felt a twinge of pity mingling with her unease. There was something oddly childlike about this barrel-chested man with a convict's shaven head and bruised eyes. Right now he looked lost and utterly confused.

"I've never seen the ocean!" he blurted. His eyes fixed imploringly on the radio, as though he expected it to argue with him. "Never!"

Kathryn tried not to smile. "It's an advertisement, Mr. Cole," she explained gently. "You do understand that, don't you? It's not really a special message to you."

Cole sank back into his seat. "You used to call me 'James,'" he murmured.

"You'd prefer that?" Kathryn's hands tightened on the wheel. "James, you don't really have a gun, do you?"

Outside, endless lines of gas stations, strip malls, condominiums swept by. The commercial ended, and the opening strains of "Blueberry Hill" rose from the speakers. Cole said nothing. When Kathryn checked the mirror, she saw him sitting entranced, mouth agape and eyes wide.

"*I found my thri—ill . . .*" Fats Waller moaned. Cole rammed into the front seat, reaching for the volume.

"I'm gonna make this louder!" he yelled. "*I love* twentieth-century music! Hearing music and *breathing air!*"

Kathryn watched incredulously as he slid across the backseat and hammered at the window control. A rush of cold air filled the car, but Cole only laughed delightedly, sticking his head out the window with his mouth open.

"*Air!*" he yelped. "*I'm breathing air!*"

Ahead a sign reared from the side of the freeway.

PHILADELPHIA—I-95 NORTH

Kathryn nibbled at her lip again and watched Cole, still reveling in the cold night air. now *what?* she thought.

"... *on Blueberry Hi—ill* ..."

Abruptly the song cut off. Cole yanked his head back in from the window, giving Kathryn an accusing look.

"*This just in from Fresno, California,*" a radio announcer pronounced in gloomy tones. "*Emergency crews are converging on a cornfield where playmates of nine-year-old Ricky Neuman say they saw him disappear right before their eyes* ..."

Cole's expression became troubled as the announcer continued.

"*Young Neuman apparently stepped into an abandoned well shaft and is lodged somewhere in the narrow one-hundred-fifty-foot pipe, possibly alive, possibly seriously injured. Playmates claim they heard him cry out faintly, but since then there has been no contact with* ..."

Cole shook his head. "'Never cry wolf!'"

Kathryn frowned, turning the radio down. "What?"

"My father told me that," Cole said rather primly. "'Never cry wolf.' Then people won't believe you if—if something really happens."

Kathryn swung the Cherokee past a bus emblazoned with posters advertising Atlantic City. "If something really happens," she repeated thoughtfully. "Like what, James?"

"Something bad." Cole yawned, running a hand across his brow. "Is that all the music? I don't want to hear this stuff."

Kathryn hit the SCAN button, glanced in the mirror to see Cole yawning again. Despite herself she felt another stab of pity for him—something she tried not to feel for most patients, especially since the warning rating she'd received from Fletcher six years before. It was one thing to make a show of empathy for the disturbed people she saw every day, quite another to grapple with unreasoned spurts of emotion like this.

But there really was something about him, she thought. For one thing, the last six years seemed to have passed over him like water. Despite a few bruises and his haggard expression, his face was as unlined as it had been when she first saw him, and his eyes—*those eyes!*—his eyes held such wounded innocence . . .

"Did—did something happen to you when you were a child?" she asked tentatively. "Something so *bad* . . . "

The radio locked into a station and Cole sat bolt upright. "Ohh, this one!" he cried. Automatically Kathryn turned up the volume.

"Since I met you baby, my whole life has changed . . . "

With an ecstatic look, Cole stuck his head out the window again. Kathryn allowed herself a small smile as she watched him fighting another yawn, his face one big loopy grin.

"Yeah, I kinda like this one, too," she murmured, but Cole didn't hear.

". . . 'cause since I met you baby, all I need is you . . ."

Cars streamed past a lonely motel bathed in pink neon. They were in the country now. Overhead the sky was flush with stars. On the western horizon the full moon poised like a kiss as the Cherokee sped on, the radio making promises it couldn't keep as Kathryn drove and Cole hung blissfully out the rear window, his weary eyes ashine, his lost heart as happy as it ever had been.

†

The next morning, Marilou Martin waited outside of Kathryn Railly's apartment building, huddling in her down parka and periodically swiping her eyes with a Kleenex. She gave an involuntary cry as a police car pulled up.

"Oh God, thank you for coming—"

The policemen nodded, tight-lipped, as Marilou followed them into the building. The super met them, a gray-faced man who opened Kathryn's apartment and then scurried back downstairs without a word. Marilou hurried into the room, bending to sweep a mewling cat into her arms.

"Oh, Carla," she murmured. "You poor thing."

The cat cried plaintively as Marilou crossed the room to Kathryn's answering machine. The police followed, eyeing the living room warily. The cat leapt from Marilou's arms and padded into the kitchen, making hungry cries. Marilou punched the answering machine and stared at it grim-faced as a single message played.

"Dr. Railly, this is Wikke from Psych Admitting. There was a guy here this afternoon looking for you. He seemed *very* agitated. We tried to keep him, but he refused, 'n I kept thinking, I *know* this guy. Then, just a few minutes ago, it came to me— It's *Cole! James Cole.* Remember him? The paranoid who pulled the Houdini back in ninety. Well, he's back and he's cuckoo and he's looking for you. I thought you oughta know."

Click. The police officers exchanged a look. Marilou turned to them, white-faced.

"It's like I told you," she said, her voice cracking. "My husband and I went to the restaurant, but she never showed. She would *never* just not show—not without calling, or—"

One of the cops broke in. "Do you happen to know the make of her car?" he asked, pulling out his notebook.

"Umm—a Cherokee. Ninety-one—no, 1992 Cherokee. Silver." Her eyes fell on the cat, piteously kneading at its empty food dish. "And that cat's starving! She would *never* neglect her cat—"

The policemen nodded. One took her arm and turned toward the door. "Would you mind coming down with us to the station for a few minutes? I'd like to get a statement."

Marilou stared at him, dazed, then nodded. "Let me call my husband first," she said, choking on her tears, and reached for the telephone.

In front of the boy, the airport concourse is empty now, except for the staggering figure of the blond man. One hand is splayed across the front of his gaudy Hawaiian shirt; blood seeps between his fingers, sends a few bright drops floating like petals onto the floor. As the boy stares, the blond woman suddenly races across the room, her mouth open as she reaches for the man. The boy shakes his head, confused, but also aroused as he knows he should not be.

Because she looks like someone, except for the honey-colored hair and briskly rouged mouth—but still he knows her, he has seen her somewhere. Her mouth is open and he can hear her now; he recognizes her voice as she races past him toward the bleeding man.

"My time machine is all ready for the experiment. All I need is somebody—is somebody—"

He woke, gasping as he sat upright. He was on a large bed, still sloppily made-up with a worn chenille spread emblazoned with a tired logo: HIGHWAYS & BYWAYS MOTEL. In front of him a snow-riddled television screen showed a wizened man with bald head and white mustache, pointing at a hole labeled TIME TUNNEL.

"—somebody—Ah, the woodpecker!"

Cole stared engrossed as Woody Woodpecker strolled across the screen.

"Yoo hoo! Woodpecker!"

"Please untie me."

Cole watched for another moment, finally turned.

"Please," Kathryn Railly repeated, exhausted.

Her jacket had been pulled backwards over her arms, the sleeves tied behind her. Her pale eyes were deeply shadowed, her hair knotted and loose to her shoulders. She looked as though she had been crying. "I'm very uncomfortable."

Cole gazed at her. He felt a slight prickling between his shoulder blades and shivered. After a moment he said, "You were in my dream just now. Your hair—"

She flinched as he reached for her face, but he only brushed a tangled lock from her forehead. "It was different. But I'm sure it was you."

Railly nodded, once, then sighed. "We dream

about what's important in our lives. And I seem to have become pretty important in yours."

Cole's hand lingered upon her brow. For a moment she thought he was going to free her, but instead he turned and stood, wincing, and limped into the bathroom, stepping between empty fast-food cartons.

Kathryn fought back a wave of despair. "What was the dream about?" she called after him.

In the door to the bathroom he stopped and looked back at her. Once more she was riveted by his eyes, that same guileless, childlike stare. "About an airport," he said. He lifted his hand and moved it slowly in front of him, like a plane. "Before everything happened. It's the same dream I always have. I'm a little kid in it."

Kathryn nodded, angling so that she could push her bound body higher onto the bed. "And I was in it?" she asked, trying to keep an unprofessional note of real curiosity from creeping into her tone. "What did I do?"

Cole stared musingly at the ceiling. "You were very upset." For a moment his gaze met hers. "You're *always* very upset in the dream, but I never knew it was you before."

Kathryn gave an exasperated moan. "It *wasn't* me before, James! It's become me *now*, because of— what's happened. *Please* untie me," she pleaded.

Cole shook his head. "No," he said vaguely, stepping into the bathroom but leaving the door open. "I think it was always you. It's very strange."

"You're flushed," Kathryn called after him—the

psychiatrist taking over for the bound and fearful woman, noting the unhealthy color of Cole's bruised face, how unnaturally brilliant his eyes were. "Your leg is hurt. And you were moaning. I think you're running a fever."

Cole reappeared, rubbing his face with a towel. Without a glance in Kathryn's direction he tossed the towel on the floor, then retrieved her wallet from where it lay on a nightstand.

"What are you doing?" demanded Kathryn. Cole pulled out several bills, dropped the wallet, and headed for the door.

"I'll be back in a minute."

"No! Don't leave me here like this!" Kathryn thrashed helplessly on the bed as the door closed behind him. Tears spilled from her eyes as the lunchtime news came on, an anchorman gazing at her from the screen with detached concern.

"... and in Fresno, California, crews continue to attempt to rescue nine-year-old Ricky Neuman ..."

"God *damn* it," Kathryn moaned, lifting herself only to fall back again.

"... playing ball with four other children when he literally disappeared off the face of the earth. Closer to home, in Baltimore, Kathryn Railly, prominent psychiatrist and the author of a newly released book on insanity, disappeared mysteriously last night after a lecture at the university."

Kathryn froze. Staring at her from the screen was a mug shot of James Cole from six years ago. The camera had trapped him with his eyes wide and vacant, mouth slightly parted to show a curve of white. Kathryn felt herself go cold, trying to think where she had seen an expression like that before—in a book, once, something she had read in college.

"A former mental patient, James Cole, is wanted for questioning regarding Dr. Railly's disappearance."

It came to her suddenly, a shaft of ice thrust down her spine: *Helter Skelter.* A courtroom photo of Charles Manson, with the same piercingly intense yet empty eyes, the mouth's same subtle curve that might have been a grimace or a sneer—or worse, a smile.

". . . authorities warn that Cole has a history of violence."

A small sound made her cry aloud. She looked up to see Cole framed in the doorway, his arms filled with bags of potato chips and cans of soda.

"Well," he said softly, staring at the haunted face filling the TV screen, "I guess it's time to check out."

The dusty roads and fields of rural Maryland rolled past as the Cherokee jounced along one back road after another. In the driver's seat Kathryn sat, stone-faced, fighting exhaustion and hoping that Cole wouldn't notice. She swatted a lank strand of hair from her eyes and glanced at him in the seat beside her. "Just because we're on back roads you think the police won't find us?"

Cole didn't look up. His finger traced a blue line on the frayed map. "We have to find, uh, Route 121A," he said absently.

Kathryn grimaced as a stone flew up and pinged the windshield. "Just because you don't see so many police cars patrolling doesn't mean they won't catch us. Sooner or later—"

Cole looked up, a shaft of morning light setting his eyes ablaze. "You still don't get it, do you?" he said softly. "There isn't any *later*."

He reached for the radio and switched it on. Jangling guitar notes filled the car. "I love music." His expression was reverent as he set aside the map and reached down beside the seat, pulling out a stack of tattered papers.

Kathryn cast a quick look at the wadded mess. "What are all those?"

"My notes. Observations. Clues."

"Clues? What kind of clues?"

Cole smoothed out a piece of newsprint covered with scrawled inscriptions. "A secret army," he said. "The Army of the Twelve Monkeys. I've told you about them. They spread the virus. I have to find them. It's my assignment."

Right, thought Kathryn, easing the car across a rutted ditch. *And I'm Mother Theresa.* "What will you do," she asked cautiously, "when you find this—secret army?"

Cole's face twisted with frustration. In his hands the worn newspaper tore along one of its many creases. "Nothing! I can't *do* anything. I just have to *locate* them, because they have the virus in its pure state, before it mutates." His voice took on the grandiose tones of a schoolkid reciting a memorized speech he's learned to love. "When I *locate* the virus, they'll send a *scientist* back here. The *scientist* will *study* the virus, and when he goes back to the present, him and all the *other* scientists will make a *cure*. Then all of us in the present, who survived, we'll be able to go back to the surface of the earth."

Somewhat breathlessly, Cole looked over at Kathryn, his eyes shining. She stared grimly out the window, her face stony with disbelief. All that pumped-up hope drained from Cole's eyes. Angrily he turned and glared out the side window, just in time to see a station wagon come barreling out from a long drive beside them. Dad driving, Mom beside him, her face bright with Sunday lipstick. In the backseat, three children in matching flannel jackets scooted over to wave at Cole. He waved back glumly, then turned to Kathryn.

"You won't think I'm crazy next month. People are going to start dying. At first the people will say it's some weird fever. Then they'll begin to catch on. They'll get it, all right."

He sat back in his seat, scowling at the radio. His expression froze as the ringing guitar chords died into the sudden hush that presaged an emergency announcement.

"We interrupt this program with a special bulletin. At least fifty police officers from three jurisdictions, apparently including special tactical unit personnel, have been mobilized to control a growing crowd of more than seven hundred onlookers in Fresno, California, where rescue operations for nine-year-old Ricky Neuman continue."

Cole let his breath out in a long, low whistle. Kathryn slowed the car to a crawl and looked at him, eyebrows raised. He shrugged sheepishly.

"I thought it was about us." He began gathering the oddments of paper that made up his clues. "I thought maybe they'd found us and arrested me or something." Kathryn just stared at him, until Cole finally looked pointedly back out at the narrow road ahead of them.

"Just a joke," he mumbled.

"So far rescue crews, including Navy sonar specialists, have been unable to determine the location of the boy in the one-hundred-fifty-foot shaft. But a TV sound man who lowered an ultrasensitive microphone into the narrow tubes claims he heard breathing sounds coming from approximately seventy feet down."

With a disgusted look, Cole punched a button, scanning until he found more music. Kathryn watched him guardedly. The Cherokee bounced down a rutted roadway, past brown, rock-strewn fields where cows grazed lazily on the frost-nipped grass.

"Does that disturb you, James?" she asked at last. "Thinking about that little boy in the well?"

Cole shook his head. He stared out at the cows, his expression unreadable. "When I was a kid, I identified with that kid, down there alone in that pipe. A hundred feet down, doesn't know if they're going to save him . . ."

Kathryn fought the urge to snap at him. "What do you mean, 'when you were a kid'?"

Cole sighed. "Never mind. It's not real. It's a hoax. A prank. He's hiding in a barn— *Hey!*"

He yelled so loudly that Kathryn sent the car careering too far to the right, nearly putting them in a ditch.

"Turn left here! *Left!*"

Gritting her teeth, Kathryn eased the car back onto the road, then turned left. In a few minutes they were on a major road once more. An hour later, she eased the Cherokee off the interstate and into Philadelphia's outer limits. In the distance the city's spires shimmered in the clear light of a snowless winter morning. Despite the cold, Cole sat beside the open window with the ferocious look of a Rottweiler straining to be loose.

"Okay," Cole said edgily. He shuffled quickly though pages until he found a small rental car agency map of the city. He puzzled over it, barking directions at Kathryn and pointing down first one industrial alley, then another, until they were cruising through a desolate part of town. A weary line of derelicts sat leaning against a long stone building, empty bottles rolling at their feet. Paper bags and Styrofoam cups rose up desultorily in the chill wind. Kathryn wrinkled her nose; Cole's open window let in the musty tang of urine, the nasty chemical smell of burning plywood. Ripped posters flapped against abandoned storefronts and rusted street signs. On a corner, a wild-eyed man in the frayed remnants of a terry cloth robe stood waving a paperback Bible.

"IN A SEASON OF GREAT PESTILENCE AND TECHNOLOGICAL HORRORS, OH YES, OH YES! THERE ARE OMENS AND DIVINATIONS!"

The Cherokee slowed nearly to a halt as Kathryn stared out Cole's side window, riveted by the gaunt figure. With his ravaged face and tangled hair and feral eyes, he was a dead ringer for the man in the engraving that graced the cover of her book. Behind him an emaciated woman squatted on the sidewalk and urinated.

"'AND ONE OF THE FOUR BEASTS GAVE UNTO THE SEVEN ANGELS SEVEN GOLDEN VIALS FULL OF THE WRATH OF GOD, WHO LIVETH FOR EVER AND EVER!' *REVELATIONS!*" Swaying back and forth the man shouted the last word triumphantly, arms raised to the distant blue sky.

"Around here somewhere," Cole murmured, bringing Kathryn back to earth. "I think if we just—"

Screeeech!

She slammed on the brakes, her heart pounding. In front of the car an old man stood with his hands drawn before his face, as though to defend himself from a blow. At his feet a half-empty trash bag billowed, spilling forth its load of empty bottles and cans.

"Christ, I almost nailed him," Kathryn gasped. "Poor guy."

She drew a few long even breaths, trying to calm herself as the scavenger gathered his recyclables and dragged the bag to safety.

"Poor!" Cole exclaimed bitterly. "He's got the sun; he's got air to breathe. He could get a whole lot poorer."

Behind them a horn blared. Kathryn looked into the rearview mirror and saw a black BMW zipping around the Cherokee. Almost immediately the BMW braked, its enraged driver leaning out the window and shouting.

"Out of the street, asshole!"

The old man stooped, his face all misery as he picked up a last bottle and the BMW roared past. Cole's bitterness turned to anger.

"All of you!" he railed, slapping his torn map against the dashboard. "You live in Eden, and you don't even notice it. You don't even see the sky. You don't . . ."

His voice broke as he let his hand dangle out the window. "You don't feel *sunshine*. You don't taste the fresh water or smell the air." As the Cherokee inched forward again, his voice became reverent. "You have *real sun-grown food*. It's all gonna be gone and— WAIT! *STOP!* HERE—*RIGHT HERE!*"

The Cherokee veered up onto the curb. It crunched to a halt and Cole leapt from the front seat, heading for a graffiti-covered wall. "Come *on!*" he yelled without looking back. Kathryn didn't move, except to reach over and pull Cole's door shut. Her hand fingered the gear shift, the gas pedal thrummed beneath her foot, but still she remained there, eyes staring straight ahead.

In thirty seconds I can be gone, she thought. *In five seconds. There's got to be a police station around here somewhere, or a pay phone. All I have to do is dial 911 and it'll all be over . . .*

She turned and watched him, told herself it was so she'd be able to give a good final description to the police. *White Caucasian male, late thirties, dressed in stained prison drabs that only accentuated his muscular frame, the determined set of his mouth and that pair of haunted eyes . . .*

He stood before the wall of a crumbling building, heedless of the garbage heaped up around his ankles. Hands splayed, he ran his fingers over the filthy moldering bricks, peeling at ragged bits of older posters and peering beneath them with ludicrous concentration. He looked like nothing so much as some dogged archaeologist at the base of a ruined temple, searching for the lost hieroglyph that would prove all his mad theories to be true. Kathryn's foot tapped the accelerator. The engine growled impatiently, but still she couldn't leave.

Cole's frantic searching slowed. His hands moved more carefully, teasing first one poster from the bricks, then another. Kathryn had a glimpse of red graffiti, not even the work of a graffiti artist but a spray-painted stencil, the paint flecked with dirt and bits of paper. Automatically, as though she were sleepwalking, she turned the ignition key to Off, slipped from the car, and walked silently to stand beside him.

"I was right." His voice shook with emotion. He did not turn to look at her. *"I was right!* They're *here!"*

Kathryn stared, first at the wall, then at Cole. Her heart flooded with pity.

Jesus Christ, he's just completely insane. She stretched a hand to touch him gently on the shoulder, but before she could, he turned.

"See!" he cried ecstatically. His finger stabbed at the filthy brick. "The Twelve Monkeys!"

Kathryn took a breath. "I see some red paint, James. Some marks."

"Marks? *Marks?"* His voice grew shrill. He ripped down more posters, tossing them aside and looking more frantically beneath. "You think they're just *marks?"*

"James—please, I want to *help* you—"

Suddenly he spun wildly, grabbed her by the wrist. Kathryn tried to pull back, but he yanked her to him, close enough that she could see his bloodshot eyes, wide now and too bright, like a meth freak coming off a three-day run.

"Don't—don't run away. Don't do anything *crazy*," he stammered. "I'll—I'll hurt somebody."

Kathryn spoke with deliberate calm, glad he couldn't feel her heart racing. "I'm not going to do anything crazy, James. But *none* of this is what you think it is—"

From behind them came a small rustle. "You can't hide from them, Bob," rasped a deep voice.

Cole whirled, dropping Kathryn's hand.

"No sir, Old Bob—don't even *try!*"

A derelict stood there, clad in a khaki trench coat stained almost black with mold and filth. Cole stared at him in horror.

That voice! The voice from his cell, croaking in the same conspiratorial tone as the ragged man pointed a warning finger at him.

"They hear everything," the derelict whispered. His rheumy eyes glittered malevolently. "They got that tracking device on you. They can find you anywhere. Anytime. *Ha!*" He cackled, his laughter tripping into a fit of coughing. Cole watched, stunned, as this urban apparition leaned closer.

The coughing died away as the derelict tapped his back jaw. "In the tooth, Bob, right?" He grinned triumphantly. "But I fooled 'em, old buddy . . . "

He opened his mouth wide, an ulcerated hole. *"No teeth!"*

With a final leer, the derelict turned and shambled off. Cole and Kathryn stared after him. Suddenly, Cole grabbed Kathryn and pulled her into an adjoining alley.

"What are you *doing?*" protested Kathryn, her purse bouncing against her side.

"They're keeping an eye on me," Cole said in a low voice. She looked at him: he was obviously shaken by the encounter with the street person.

"Who do you think is keeping an eye on you, James?"

He yanked her closer to him, the two of them foundering through a sea of plastic bags, broken glass, desiccated paper.

"The man with the voice!" Cole hissed. *"Them!* People from the present. What for?" he added in a hurt tone. "I'm doing what I'm supposed to do. They don't have to spy on me. They—"

He stopped short. Kathryn pitched forward, catching herself before she fell onto a heap of smashed beer bottles. Her purse landed in front of her. She picked it up and, when she straightened, saw Cole staring rigidly at the brick wall. Across it was drawn another red graffiti: the stenciled image of a circle inset with twelve dancing monkeys.

"They're here!" Cole's voice was jubilant. He pulled Kathryn after him and ran further down the alley, scanning the walls. She had no choice but to follow, crying out once when a twisted bit of metal slashed at her leg and watching as Cole anxiously scanned the walls for graffiti. There was plenty of that—mostly obscenities, a few wan attempts at consciousness-raising.

FREE N'BERO MAM! YES ON SARAJEVO! Kathryn looked nervously over her shoulder. The alley entrance looked very far away, a tiny bright mouth in the fetid darkness. She let out a small cry as Cole abruptly tugged her after him, into a dark and forbidding doorway. Just inside, two oblivious women leaned against the rotting sill, sucking at crack pipes.

"James, *no.*" With all her strength Kathryn pulled herself upright, resisting him. "We shouldn't be here—"

Ignoring her he pulled her through the door. Something scuttled into the shadows. Beneath her feet the ground was spongy, heaped with decaying clothing. She almost gagged on the overwhelming smell of putrid water and the burning reek of crack. Cole barged on like a man possessed, finally stopping in the gloomy hallway. In front of them broken drywall held another stencil of the twelve dancing monkeys, this one apparently painted with a brush. Red paint had dried in long oozing lines beneath the circle and splotched onto the floor, forming a trail. Kathryn looked at the floor, then slowly raised her head. Her eyes widened.

"James," she whispered hoarsely.

Scarcely ten feet away, two shadowy figures kicked at a third figure hunched over on the floor. At the sound of Kathryn's voice one looked up and without a word nudged his partner. The two men took in first Kathryn, then Cole. They exchanged a glance, and soundlessly started toward them.

"James!" Kathryn repeated frantically. *"We have to go back.* Those men—"

Too late. "Hey, buddy," the taller man said. Startled, Cole blinked stupidly at him, as the other man lunged for Kathryn's purse and grabbed it from her.

"No!" she screamed.

With a grunt Cole tried to grab it back, but—

Whack! Something smashed across his cheek. Kathryn cried out again, more desperately this time. Dazed, Cole drew a hand across his face, stared at blood staining his fingers. Before he could react something cold and hard ground into his other cheek. Looking out of the corner of his eyes, Cole saw a tin-bright pistol, so shiny and cheap looking it was like a kid's toy.

Biting back a cry, Kathryn turned to run. She took only two steps before the second man knocked her roughly to the ground.

"Stick around, bitch," he said, smiling. Looming above her he began to unzip his fly. Kathryn looked around wildly, saw Cole drop to his knees.

"Please!" he whimpered, clutching pathetically at handfuls of moldering paper. "Please don't hurt me!"

The man stared down at him. He stepped closer to Cole and kicked him contemptuously. He drew his foot back for a second kick when Cole suddenly lunged upward, wrapping his arms around the man's calves. In one fluid motion he lifted the man from the ground.

The pistol fired, its echo nearly drowning Cole's enraged roar. He staggered forward and rammed the man into the brick wall. There was a crack like stone hitting stone as the man's head smashed against brick, then lolled onto his breast. The man fell into a heap, the pistol dropping from his limp hand.

"Uh, later, lady." The second man hastily zipped his fly. Before he could run Cole was on top of him, fists crushing into him again and again, savagely. The man staggered backward, bloody and dazed. Kathryn watched dumbfounded. Cole's fist crashed into the man's jaw one last time. Cole turned back to his first assailant, saw him reaching weakly for the pistol.

Without a word Cole kicked him viciously in the jaw. Kathryn covered her mouth as the man's head whipped back.

"Oh, God," she whispered. She heard a small *pop*, as though a dry stick had been stepped on. The man collapsed against the wall. She glanced furtively behind her and saw the second man running haphazardly down the hallway, one arm flapping uselessly at his side. When she looked up, Cole was standing there above her in the blue-tinged darkness. He no longer looked merely insane, or even dangerous. With his bloody face, eyes staring grimly at her, and the cheap pistol gripped in his immense hand, he looked positively lethal.

"Are you hurt?" he asked, shoving the gun into a pocket. He sounded as though it pained him to talk.

Kathryn stumbled to her feet. "Uh, no. Yes—" She glanced down quickly at her torn skirt, blood threading the cuffs of her blouse. "I mean, just some scrapes—"

He wasn't listening. Instead, Cole was bent over the motionless body, quickly going through the man's pockets. He held up a wallet, then a handful of bullets; he tossed aside a set of keys and shoved the other items into his own pocket.

"Is he—alive?" breathed Kathryn.

Cole looked at her with cold eyes. "Come on." He stood, yanked her roughly after him. Kathryn glanced back and for the first time saw the other man's eyes, wide open and glazed with a fine spray of dirt.

"Oh, Jesus, James! You *killed* him—"

Cole's icy gaze never left her. "I did him a favor. Now come on."

He pulled her down the hall, past another lurid crimson circle with its crude grinning monkeys. Ahead of them a faint glimmer of light showed through the murk, giving a sanguine glow to the trail of spattered red paint that stretched before them.

"You didn't have a gun before, did you?" Kathryn asked, her voice dead.

"I've got one now," Cole replied, and dragged her toward the light.

Outside the winter sun shone thin and bright onto another desolate city block. Cole kept a tight hold of Kathryn's hand; she ran panting after him, his head bent as he followed scattered drops of red paint. The block's few denizens ignored them, street people and a hollow-eyed woman who shouted curses as she banged her head against a lamppost. Cole loped on and Kathryn struggled to keep up with him, until finally they turned a corner and were both brought up short at the sight of the same ranting evangelist, standing now on a pile of broken cinderblocks and shouting hoarsely at the pale sky.

"'And the seventh angel poured out his vial into the air; and there came—' *You! You!*"

With an inhuman shriek the man stiffened, then pointed wildly at Cole. "*YOU'RE ONE OF US!*"

Kathryn shuddered, but Cole only focused on the obscure paint trail, almost hidden now beneath the heavy patina of grime and trash that covered the sidewalk. It was still there, faint but perceptible, and Cole walked quickly, head bent, his free hand slapping distractedly at his side.

All of a sudden he halted. Kathryn drew up beside him, exhausted.

"*Now* what—"

They were in front of what had once been a butcher shop, a wooden storefront with loose clapboards and cracked windows now covered with lurid animal rights posters. Atop the building a faded sign still bore the legend:

IACONO'S
FINE MEATS & POULTRY
WE DO KOSHER

A newer sign, hand-painted in the same garish crimson as the now-faded paint trail, read FREEDOM FOR ANIMALS ASSOCIATION. The front door was heavy plate glass, broken and clumsily repaired with duct tape. Inside, three people sat in folding chairs in a cluttered, dingy room. Their voices filtered through the broken glass, arguing as they collated papers from a heap on the floor.

"You know, Fale, this would've been, like, a whole lot easier if we just had Kinko's do it," a young woman whined. She had long, stringy hair, dyed black, a ring through her nose, and purplish lipstick. "'Cause then—"

Beside her a deathly pale boy rolled his eyes. "Like, *right*, Bee," he said, aping her nasal voice. "But we like don't have any *money*." In the chair next to his, a tall muscular young man with a shaved head and a lizard tattoo nodded earnestly.

"Yeah," he agreed. "And not only that—"

Keeping his grip on Kathryn's wrist, Cole shoved the door open and stepped inside. The sound of pouring rain surrounded him. On the cracked tile walls hung posters showing the bloodied forms of cats and chimpanzees, their eyes wide and glazed with fear. The floor was covered with flyers and brochures depicting more atrocities. As Cole and Kathryn stepped over cartons and books, the three activists looked up in surprise. On the wall behind them hung a huge poster proclaiming ANIMALS HAVE SOULS, TOO. Cole looked around, frowning, as the sound of rain grew louder; then started when a tremendous thunderclap shook the small room. A jungle bird screamed. Cole pulled Kathryn closer to him, glancing uneasily over his shoulder.

"Uh, can we help you?" Fale blinked rapidly, like a creature unaccustomed to daylight.

Cole hesitated, confused. The sound of rain abated, replaced by the sudden trumpeting roar of an elephant.

"It's all right, James," Kathryn murmured. "It's just a tape." She pointed to a tape deck under a sign advertising THE TRUE MUSIC OF THE WORLD.

Cole nodded, swallowing nervously, and turned his attention back to the three activists. "I, uh, I'm looking for the, uh, the Army of the Twelve Monkeys."

Fale glanced at Bee, then at the skinhead, giving them pointed looks. "Um, Teddy?" he asked, raising his eyebrows.

Monkeys started chattering on the tape as the skinhead stood. He was huge, taller than Cole, his powerful arms flexing in his sleeveless T-shirt. "We don't know anything about any 'Army of the Twelve Monkeys,' so why don't you and your friend disappear, okay?" He smiled menacingly, gesturing at the door.

A lion roared as Cole backed away, pulling Kathryn after him. "I just need some information."

Teddy shook his head, a little plastic gorilla dangling from one ear. "Didn't you hear me? We're not—"

He froze as Cole pointed the pistol at him. Kathryn shook her head and cried, "James, no! Don't hurt them—"

She turned to the activists, Cole's hand still gripping her tightly. "Please, I'm a psychiatrist. Just do whatever he tells you to do," she begged. "He's—upset. *Disturbed.* Please! He's dangerous—just cooperate."

A tiger snarled, monkeys chattered wildly as Teddy backed away. Behind him Fale dug furiously in his jeans pocket.

"What do you want—money? We only have a few bucks—"

Cole shook his head, suddenly confident again. "I told you what I want." He let go of Kathryn's hand and waved the pistol at her threateningly. "Lock the door!"

Kathryn took a breath. "James, why don't we——"

"Lock it *now!*"

She hurried to the door. On the floor, the girl Bee turned to Fale and whimpered, "I *told* you that fuckhead Goines would get us into something like this."

Fale looked like he was going to slap her. "Shut up!"

"*Goines?*" Cole stared at them.

"*Jeffrey* Goines?" repeated Kathryn in amazement.

Cole pointed the gun first at Teddy, then the other activists. "Okay," he said a little breathlessly. "We have some stuff to talk about. Go——" He gestured at a door in the back of the room. "Let's go."

The door led to an abandoned meat locker. Cole poked among boxes and trash cans until he found some stereo wire, then ordered Kathryn to hog-tie the three of them in the middle of the floor.

"All right," Cole announced, keeping the gun trained on Teddy. "Now tell me about the Twelve Monkeys."

They told him, the three of them interrupting each other, momentarily falling silent when Cole asked them to repeat something.

". . .then, Jeffrey becomes like this—*big star . . .*" Fale explained eagerly. "The media latch onto him because he's picketing his own father, this famous Nobel prize-winning virologist. You musta seen all that on TV."

Without looking up Cole said, "No. I don't watch TV." He continued rummaging through a stack of papers near the door while Kathryn watched helplessly. Suddenly he frowned, picking up a photograph and staring at it intently. The image was of a distinguished-looking man being escorted through a mob of raging activists by a phalanx of riot police. The caption read, "Dr. Leland Goines."

"The slide," he murmured. Then, turning to Fale, "Is this him? Dr. Goines?"

Fale nodded. "That's him."

On the floor beside him, Bee wriggled despondently. "What are you going to do with us?"

Cole ignored her, scrutinizing the photo. "Tell me more about Jeffrey," he said in a low voice.

Fale glanced at his cohorts and shrugged hopelessly. "Jeffrey started getting bored with the shit we do—picketing, leafleting, letter-writing stuff. He said we were—" Fale paused as Teddy watched him grimly "—ineffectual liberal jerkoffs. *He* wanted to do guerrilla actions to 'educate' the public."

Slowly Cole set down the photo of Leland Goines, picked up a magazine clipping showing horrified senators standing on their desks as rattlesnakes slithered along the Senate floor. He held it up questioningly to Fale.

"Yeah." Fale nodded, grinning faintly. "That's when he let a hundred snakes loose in the Senate."

"But we weren't into that kind of stuff," Teddy blurted. "It's counterproductive, we told him."

Fale nodded. "So he and eleven others split off and became this underground . . . 'army.'"

"The Army of the Twelve Monkeys," said Cole.

For the first time Bee piped in. "They started planning a 'Human Hunt.'"

"They bought stun guns and nets and bear traps," Teddy went on. "They were gonna go to Wall Street and trap lawyers and bankers."

"But they didn't do it," said Bee. "They didn't do any of it."

Teddy shook his head. "Yeah. Just like always, Mr. Big Shot sold his friends out!"

Cole fixed his burning gaze on Fale. "What's that mean?"

"He goes on TV," Fale explained quickly, "gives a news conference, tells the whole world he just realized his daddy's experiments are vital for humanity and that the use of animals is absolutely necessary and that he, Jeffrey Goines, from now on, is going to personally supervise the labs to make sure all the little animals aren't going to suffer." Fale finished and stared up at Cole, his pale face paper-white. "Can we—do you think you could let us go now?"

Cole turned away, bent back over a cardboard box, and started throwing papers out of it. After a moment he held up a Rolodex. "What's this?"

The three activists exchanged worried looks. "Uh, that's a Rolodex," said Teddy. "You know, for phone numbers?"

Cole flipped through the little index cards, stopped and peered at one. "Jeffrey Goines," he read aloud. He stood and crossed to the hog-tied activists. "Which one of you has a car?"

Silence.

"I said, which one of—"

"Me!" broke in Fale. He wriggled sideways, ducking his head to indicate his jeans pocket. "Keys in there—an old Jag—"

Cole took the keys. Without a backward glance he strode to where Kathryn crouched in a corner and grabbed her. "Come on."

"Where are you going?" wailed Bee. "You can't just *leave* us . . . "

Kathryn shot her one last pitying look. *Oh yes he can*, she thought, and followed Cole outside.

They found Fale's car, a battered Jaguar covered with bumper stickers and painted slogans—I BRAKE FOR ANIMALS, FREE THE ANIMALS! WOULD YOU LET A MINK WEAR YOUR SKIN? Cole shoved Kathryn inside, then got into the seat beside her. She slid the key into the ignition. There was a grinding noise, and the car lurched forward.

She drove through midday traffic, staring grimly out the windshield. The radio played moody country and western music, a few mournful ballads. Finally, in a tight voice she said, "Dr. Goines isn't going to be someone you can just barge in on, James. He's very well known; he's been the target of animal rights protesters; he's going to have security guards, gates, alarms. It's—this is insane!"

Cole said nothing, just looked at the map in his lap, moving his head in time to the music. His face was feverish, beaded with sweat. Beside the map, the Rolodex flapped open to a much-worn card:

JEFFREY GOINES C/O DR. LELAND GOINES, 27 OUTER-
BRIDGE ROAD.

"And those kids," Kathryn went on, gaining steam.
"They could *die* in that locker!"

Cole glanced out the window at passing cars: families returning home from church, truckers, two boys
on a motorcycle, a van full of laughing children.

"All I see are dead people," he said, his eyes dull.
"Everywhere. What's three more?"

Kathryn fought the urge to shout at him, instead
tightened her hands on the steering wheel. *Get it
together, Railly*, she thought. She stopped at a red
light, watched a young girl push a baby across the
street in a stroller. When the light changed the Jag
lunged forward again. She decided to take a different
tack.

"You know his son, Jeffrey, don't you?" she asked.
"When you were at County Hospital six years ago.
Jeffrey Goines was a patient there for a couple of
weeks."

Cole continued to peruse the map. "The guy was
a—a total fruitcake."

"And he told you his father was a famous virologist."

Cole's finger traced a black line with the words
OUTERBRIDGE ROAD. "No," he said, shaking his head.
"He told me his father was *God.*"

Abruptly, the twanging of a banjo gave way to a
news bulletin.

*"This just in. Police confirm that prominent psychiatrist
and author Dr. Kathryn Railly has been abducted by a
dangerous mental patient, James—"*

Silently Cole switched the station. Shifting uncomfortably in his seat, he checked the road map against the road signs flashing past. Kathryn saw him wince with pain as he shifted his leg. For the first time she noticed a dark stain beneath the knee.

"What's the matter with your leg?"

Cole shrugged. "I got shot."

"Shot!" She looked aside at him, took in how flushed he was, the sheen of sweat on his face, his arms, his neck. "Who shot you?"

"It was some kind of war." For a moment she thought he was going to elaborate, but instead he said, "Never mind. You wouldn't believe me—hey! What're you doing?"

The car swung into the right lane as she put on the turn signal. Just ahead on the highway was a gas station, flanked by a convenience store. "We don't need gas!" Cole snapped, leaning over to check the gas gauge.

"I thought you didn't know how to drive."

"I said I was too *young* to drive," Cole said warningly. He put his hand on the wheel. "I didn't say I was stupid."

Kathryn's foot tapped at the brake as they approached the Sundry Store by the gas station. "Look, James. This can't go on. You're not well. You're burning with fever. And I'm a doctor—I need supplies."

The Jag idled and she turned to look at him, her eyes pleading with him to trust her. "Please, James?" she whispered.

He gazed back at her: those pale eyes that hadn't

seen sleep in two days now, her hair falling limply across her smooth forehead. Slowly he let go of the wheel and leaned back in his seat.

"All right," he murmured, closing his eyes for a moment. "All right."

Late afternoon found them in the woods some forty miles north. Pale sunlight filtered through the bare limbs of oak trees. The air smelled sweetly of fallen leaves, crushed acorns, the faint clean scent of running water. Overhead, a skein of wild geese made their way southward, their cries hanging in the air long after they were out of sight.

Beside the car, Cole leaned against a granite boulder, staring at the sky. He wore only his frayed flannel shirt and boxer shorts; his trousers hung on the Jag's open door beside a plastic bag of gauze and surgical tape. Kathryn stooped in front of him, adjusting a bandage on his thigh. Her touch was sure but gentle; he remembered that she had said she was a doctor, a real doctor.

"There. You shouldn't put your weight on it." Kathryn straightened. She held up the bullet for his inspection, then wrapped it in gauze and stuck it in her pocket. Cole glanced at her, then looked back up at the sky.

"I love seeing the sun." He blinked, relishing the wan warmth that touched his cheeks despite the afternoon's chill. Then with a sigh he leaned forward. He tugged his pants from the car door, struggling to get into them, and almost fell.

"Wait—let me help you."

Kathryn put an arm around him, pulling him to her as she tugged the pants over his legs. Cole leaned closer to her, closing his eyes.

"You smell so good," he murmured.

She paused and looked into his face. His eyes opened and she found herself staring into them, seeing the reflection of branches, sky, a tiny sun, her own face. Her mouth went dry and she felt herself flush as he reached his hand out and touched her cheek, stroking a tendril of dark hair.

"You—you have to give yourself up, you know," she said, her voice breaking.

Cole blinked. His eyes grew hard, all the reflected wonder fading from them as he grit his teeth.

"James, please," she went on pleadingly. "If you would just—"

She broke off, shocked, as his hand closed around her wrist so tightly that she gasped.

"I'm really sorry," he said. His voice was utterly devoid of warmth as he turned and pushed her back into the car. "But I have to do this. I have a mission."

Moments later the Jag coughed to life once more and edged out of the clearing, back onto the road.

It was night when they found Outerbridge Road. They drove past dairy farms and fallow cornfields, a few farmhouses with lights burning yellow in the early winter evening. Finally they reached a high stone wall whose gates read NUMBER 27. Well back from the road, a brightly lit Craftsman-style mansion sat amidst rolling lawns and bare maple trees. The driveway and the road were lined with luxury cars.

Cole could see several uniformed security guards strolling down the drive, holding walkie-talkies and waving to guests.

"Keep going," he said tightly, and the Jag moved on.

They drove another half mile or so. Then, "Here," Cole commanded. "Go left."

Kathryn shook her head. "Left? There's nothing but—"

"*Turn.*"

At the side of the road was a small clearing that extended a good ways into the wood. A faint glimmer of moonlight touched the slender shadows of aspen and sumac. With a groan, the Jag rolled off the blacktop and onto pitted ground, crawled along until Cole said, "Stop. Right here."

Kathryn turned off the ignition. "You know, you really can't—"

But he was already outside, limping as he raced to the driver's door. He yanked it open and pulled Kathryn out, palming the Jag's keys.

"What are you *doing?!*"

Silently he dragged her to the back of the Jag and pulled the trunk open.

"No—James, *no!*"

Still silent, he grabbed her and pushed her in, slamming the trunk closed. Her muffled cries followed him as he began limping out of the clearing.

"*James!*"

He halted, panting, and looked back; then, his fists clenching and unclenching, he slowly and purposefully returned to the car.

A short while later he made his way back down the road. After he'd gone about a hundred yards, he swung over the wall and cut through the woods, moving stealthily through the shadows until he saw below him the mansion's circular drive. More cars were parked here, and two well-built men in black business suits patrolled them vigilantly, pausing every now and then to have a cigarette. Cole waited until they were on the far end of the lot, then ran in an awkward half-crouch from the cover of the bare trees, grimacing as his injured leg banged against a stone. A minute later he was rolling beneath a red Mercedes, his heart hammering inside him and his breath coming in hard gasps.

"They find him?"

Cole sprawled beneath the car. Gravel dug into his chest and arms, lodged painfully around Kathryn Railly's bandage. A few feet away, close enough that he could have grabbed him if he wanted to, one of the men paused. Cole watched as the man's shiny black shoes kicked idly at the gravel, then ground out a smoldering cigarette.

"Find who?" A second pair of feet joined the first.

"That kid. The one in the pipe."

Harsh laughter from the second man. "You believe this? They're dropping a monkey down there with a miniature infrared camera strapped on him and a roast beef sandwich wrapped in tin foil."

The other man guffawed. "You're making that up!"

Bruce Willis stars as James Cole, a prisoner being used for
critical time-travel experiments.

Cole is interrogated by six scientists trying to isloate a deadly virus from the past.

Cole gathers specimens for the scientists in a devastated Philadelphia.

Kathryn Railly (Madeline Stowe) is a psychiatrist unsure whether to believe Cole's outrageous tale of time travel and impending diaster.

Locked in a psychiatric hospital, Cole meets an inmate, Jeffrey Goines (Brad Pitt) with prophetic warnings of his own.

Brad Pitt plays Jeffery Goines, charismatic lunatic son of famous scientist, Dr. Leland Goines.

Cole fights to find the Army of 12 Monkeys, a group of insane eco-terrorists, even if it means another trip through time.

Cole is wrenched back to the future.

Cole and Railly race against time to locate the source of the
deadly virus.

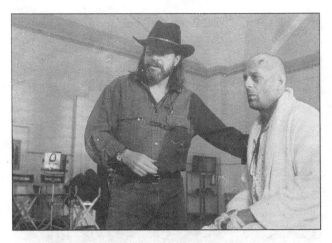

Terry Gilliam and Bruce Willis on the set.

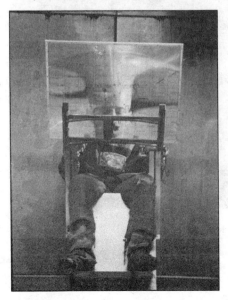

One final trip.

James Cole—no choices remain.

"I shit you not." Cole let his breath out as the voices began to recede and the two pairs of feet faded into the shadows at the other end of the drive. "Man, life is weird! A monkey and a sandwich."

Without a sound, Cole rolled out from under the Mercedes and under the car in front of it. His eyes remained fixed on the small bright oblong that was the side entrance to the mansion. He never saw his pistol, lying in the gravel beneath the red Mercedes behind him.

Inside his father's house, Jeffrey Goines sat grinning in the formal dining room, listening to his father speak. Around him were forty-odd other guests, elegantly attired in black tie and evening gowns, the sea of black broken here and there by a sequined dress, the crimson slash of a cummerbund. Jeffrey took another sip of champagne and gazed longingly at the untouched dessert in front of the woman beside him. Some captain of industry's anorexic trophy wife, an aspiring model who might weigh one hundred pounds, if you counted the rack of diamonds around her neck. He toyed with the idea of just *taking* her plate—it was sinful, really, to waste chocolate profiteroles like that, not to mention Raoul's sublime raspberry trifle.

A wave of laughter brought his attention back to the head of the table where Leland Goines stood. He was truly an imposing figure in his tux, over six feet tall and broad-shouldered, with silvery hair and ice-blue eyes. Leland waited until the laughter subsided, then went on in his rich, deep voice.

"Would that I could enjoy this opulent dinner and this excellent and stimulating company for itself, with no sense of purpose," he said, gesturing grandly around the table. "But, alas, I am burdened with the sense that with all this excess of public attention and this cacophony of praise, there comes great responsibility. Indeed, I practically feel a soapbox growing under my feet whenever I stand for more than a few seconds."

More knowing laughter from the guests. Jeffrey bared his teeth in a false smile.

"Oh, ha," he said, and deftly speared a profiterole from his neighbor's plate.

"The dangers of science are a time-worn threat," Dr. Goines continued, "from Prometheus stealing fire from the gods to the Cold War era of the Dr. Strangelove terror. "

From a doorway at the far end of the room entered a scowling man in a black suit. His gaze darted across the long table, taking in the rows of rapt faces. After a minute he sighted the object of his search.

"Mr. Goines," a low voice came from behind Jeffrey.

Jeffrey hastily swallowed his chocolate, dabbing his mouth with a napkin as he craned his neck to see who was calling him.

"Yeah?"

The black-clad man bent to whisper in Jeffrey's ear. At the head of the table, Leland Goines gathered steam, his voice rising and falling in evangelical fervor.

"But never before—not even at Los Alamos, when

the scientists made bets on whether their first atomic bomb test would wipe out New Mexico—never before has science given us so much reason to fear the power we have at hand."

Now it was Jeffrey's turn to scowl, staring in disbelief at the man standing beside him. *"What* are you talking about?" he said loudly. "What friend? I'm not expecting anyone."

Heads turned to see what the disturbance was. Dr. Goines frowned, irritated at being interrupted. He raised a hand and went on, even louder than before.

"Current genetic engineering as well as my own work with viruses has presented us with powers as terrifying as any— "

With an apologetic look at the woman beside him, Jeffrey got up from his seat. "This is ridiculous," he grumbled. His chair squeaked noisily and he knocked over a dessert spoon. "My father is making a *major address.*"

He followed the man into a dimly lit hallway leading to the library. "Plus," Jeffrey went on heatedly, "you Secret Service guys, I thought it was your *job* to screen people."

The agent stared resolutely ahead of them. "Normally if we caught a guy sneaking around like this with no ID, we'd bust his ass, excuse the French. But this one said he knows *you*—" the agent smirked "—and, since you seem to have had some, uh, unusual, uh—*associates*—we certainly didn't want to arrest one of your, uh, *closest pals.*"

They found the library. Its heavy mahogany doors were open, showing off a man-high arrangement of oriental lilies in glowing shades of orange, crimson, yellow. Only a few ambient lights were on, illuminating a gallery of small Illuminist paintings, a glass case holding rare books. In a leather wingback chair by the fireplace sat James Cole, staring at the floor. His arms and flannel shirt were smeared with dirt and car grease. Behind him another black-suited agent stood guard. Jeffrey crossed the room, absently fiddling with his bow tie. He gave Cole a cursory glance, then turned to go.

"Never saw him before in my life," he said, stifling a yawn, and shot the two agents a parting look. "Now I'm going to go back and listen to my father's very eloquent discourse on the perils of science *while you torture this intruder to death*—or whatever it is you guys do," he finished, stepping out the door.

Cole lifted his head. "I'm here about some monkeys."

Jeffrey froze. For a moment he was silent. Then:

"Excuse me—what did you say?"

"Monkeys," Cole repeated. He got to his feet. "Twelve of them."

Jeffrey frowned, studying Cole. Suddenly, with a cry, he ran across the room and embraced him.

"Arnold! *Arnold.*"

Cole looked at him in astonishment. So did the two Secret Service agents. Jeffrey drew back, his hands still on Cole's arms, and considered him more carefully. "My God, Arnie, what's happened to you? You look like shit!"

One of the agents eyed Cole dubiously. "You *know* this man?"

Jeffrey glared at him. "Of *course* I know him. What do you think—I act like this to *strangers*?" He turned back to Cole. "Christ, Arnie, it's black tie! I mean, I said 'drop by,' but, like, this is Dad's big 'do'! VIPs, senators, Secret Service—the whole ball of wax."

He threw an arm over Cole's shoulder, nearly sending Cole off balance, and started leading him to the door. The two agents exchanged narrow-eyed looks.

"Arnie?" one repeated.

Jeffrey gave him a fetching smile. "Arnold Pettibone. Old Arnie Pettibone," he said fondly, punching Cole's arm. "Used to be my best friend. Still is." He pinched Cole's cheek. "What've you lost, Arnie—forty pounds? No wonder I don't know you. You hungry?"

With a grin Jeffrey steered him into the hall. Cole limped beside him, occasionally putting a hand against the wall to keep himself straight and leaving a trail of dark smudges. "We got all *kinds* of food," Jeffrey babbled cheerily. "Lots of dead cow, dead lamb, dead pig. Real *killer* feast we're putting on tonight!"

The Secret Service agents watched them go down the hall, the disheveled Cole supported by Jeffrey in his new tux.

"These people—all of 'em—are true weirdoes!"

The other agent nodded, unamused. "I'm gonna call in a description of this 'Pettibone' character. You go keep an eye on him. Make sure he doesn't do one of the guests with a fork."

At the end of the hallway, guests were pouring

from the dining hall. Cole stared at them with rising panic, but Jeffrey waved at them gleefully.

"Hey, nice ta see ya! Lookin' good! Hi, there. Yes, it *has* been a long time . . ."

He maneuvered Cole adroitly through the crowd toward a grand, sweeping staircase that circled up through the mansion's three stories. Behind them, moving with great care through the elegant mob, a Secret Service agent observed the two warily.

". . . yeah, it's been a slice! Ta, darling!" Jeffrey wiggled the fingers of his free hand at a departing guest, then turned his megawatt gaze on Cole. "County Hospital, right?" he whispered excitedly. "1990. The 'Immaculate Escape' . . . am I right?"

Cole shook his head. "Listen to me. I can't *do* anything about what you're going to do. I can't *change* anything. I can't *stop* you. I just want some information."

Jeffrey nodded eagerly. *"We need to talk,"* he said, his voice suddenly ripe with conspiracy. "Come on. Upstairs—"

A passing guest eyed them curiously as Jeffrey led Cole up the grand staircase. Jeffrey stopped, flinging his arms up in a triumphant "V" for victory.

"I am a new person!" he cried. "I'm completely adjusted! Witness the tux—" He tugged proudly at his lapels. *"Designer."* The guest hurried in the opposite direction, and Jeffrey lowered his head beside Cole's.

"Who chattered?" he whispered. "Bruhns? Weller?"

Cole's burning eyes were as intense as Jeffrey's. "I

just need to have access to the pure virus, that's all!" he said desperately. "For the future!"

Jeffrey paused, did a double take. He narrowed his eyes, taking in Cole's frantic expression, his torn clothes and injured leg.

"Come on, follow me," he said at last, shaking his head. "You don't look so good."

Cole let Jeffrey lead him, but cast frequent looks backward, to where the crowd was thinning out. Near the dining room door the two Secret Service agents stood, staring at Cole with undisguised interest. He took a deep breath and turned back to Jeffrey.

"I need to know where it is and exactly what it is."

Jeffrey nodded excitedly. "I get it! This is your old plan, right?"

"Plan?" Cole's brow furrowed. "What are you talking about?"

"Remember? We were in the dayroom, watching TV, and you were all upset about the desecration of the planet. And you said to me, 'Wouldn't it be *great* if there was a germ or a virus that could wipe out mankind and leave the plants and animals just as they are?' You do remember that, don't you?"

Cole frowned, swiped at a bead of sweat trickling down his face. "You're—you're trying to confuse me."

Jeffrey moved faster up the stairs, his voice rising. "And that's when I told you my father was this famous virologist and you said, 'Hey, he could *make* a germ and we could steal it!'"

Cole grabbed him, so that Jeffrey thudded into the banister. "The thing mutates!" he said through

129

clenched teeth. "We live underground! The world belongs to the dogs and cats. *We're* like moles or worms. All we want to do is study the original—"

A steely grip suddenly locked onto Cole's shoulder and spun him around.

"Okay, take it easy. We know who you are, Mr. Cole."

The second agent appeared beside the first. "Let's go somewhere and talk this thing over, okay? Just come with us—"

Eyes wide, Jeffrey backed away from them. "You're right! Absolutely right! He's a nut case, totally deranged. Delusional. Paranoid." His voice cracked as it rose dangerously. "HIS PROCESSOR'S ALL FUCKED UP, HIS INFORMATION TRAY IS JAMMED—"

The two agents hoisted Cole between them like a trapped animal. They carried him downstairs, Jeffrey snapping at his heels, yelling so that the remaining guests stopped and stared amazed at the weird little tableau on the grand staircase.

"YOU KNOW WHAT IT IS, 'THE ARMY OF THE TWELVE MONKEYS?' IT'S A COLLECTION OF NATURE KOOKS WHO RUN A STORE DOWNTOWN! SPACE-CASE DO-GOODERS SAVING RAIN FORESTS! I HAVE NOTHING TO DO WITH THOSE BOZOS ANYMORE! I QUIT BEING THE RICH KID FALL GUY FOR A BUNCH OF INEFFECTUAL BANANAS! SO MUCH FOR YOUR *GRAND PLOT!*"

Cole writhed in his captors' grasp and looked

behind him to where Jeffrey stood, every hair in place, his beautiful new tuxedo gleaming, his blue eyes aglow. He appeared utterly confident, his disdainful expression telling Cole everything.

He's a nut case, totally deranged. Delusional. Paranoid. . . .

Cole shook his head, his mouth dry. *No! I'm not crazy, I can't be—*

"Take it easy, Mr. Goines, we've got him," one of the agents called back. "Everything's—"

"MY FATHER HAS BEEN WARNING PEOPLE ABOUT THE DANGERS OF EXPERIMENTATION WITH VIRUSES AND DNA FOR YEARS! YOU'VE PROCESSED THAT INFORMATION THROUGH YOUR ADDLED PARANOID INFRASTRUCTURE AND—LO AND BEHOLD! *I'M FRANKENSTEIN!* AND 'THE ARMY OF THE TWELVE MONKEYS' BECOMES SOME SORT OF SINISTER REVOLUTIONARY CABAL! *THIS MAN IS TOTALLY BATSHIT!* YOU KNOW WHERE HE THINKS HE COMES FROM?"

Without warning, Cole ducked, elbowing one agent and sending him flying. He wrenched free from the other and stumbled wildly down the stairs, heading for the front door. But Cole could just make out the figure of a third agent, racing toward him from a knot of confused guests. Grabbing at a side table for support, Cole propelled himself through the small crowd of astonished partygoers, limping as he burst through a doorway into the kitchen. An agent followed, shoving his way past guests and slamming the kitchen door open as he barged in.

"Did a man just come through here, limping?"

Several servants backed against the wall, shaking their heads. A heavyset man in a cook's toque sat unperturbed in a captain's chair, holding a brandy snifter before his nose. Above him, on a shelf between rows of cookbooks and herb vinegars, a small television blared. It showed a tiny monkey, wide-eyed and trembling in terror, clutching a small parcel as it was lowered into a narrow pipe.

"*. . . assure us there will be no negative psychological effects to the monkey . . .*"

"Anybody see someone running through here?" the agent repeated, yelling.

In his chair, the cook took another sip of his post-prandial brandy and shook his head stubbornly. "Nope. And if you ask me, that monkey's gonna eat that goddamn sandwich himself."

The other servants stared at him. The agent shook his head, while the TV image switched to a black-and-white newspaper photo of Kathryn Railly, smiling as she signed a stack of books.

"*This just in: Police say that the body of a woman found strangled in the Knutson State Park area could be kidnap victim Dr. Kathryn Railly.*"

With a disgusted look, the agent raced to the window and flung it open.

Outside, another agent prowled cautiously among the rows of Mercedes, BMWs, Range Rovers, and Porsches. At the sound of the window opening he whirled, pistol drawn, but relaxed when he saw his colleague peering out from the mansion. He held out his hands, palms up, to indicate he'd had no sign of Cole.

Relieved, the first agent withdrew from the window. He turned to see the kitchen staff engrossed once more in the eleven o'clock news.

"Earlier in the day, police located Railly's abandoned car not far from a building where three animal rights activists were found bound and gagged."

"Any sign of him?"

The agent shook his head as his partner strode into the room. "Nothing."

His partner slammed his fist into his thigh. "He can't just disappear!"

"Damn straight," the cook muttered, pouring himself another inch of Rémy Martin. "Eat that sandwich and get his ass *outta* there."

In the darkness, the trees crackled and hissed. Stray branches raked his face as he ran, gasping. Once he nearly fell, but caught himself by grabbing a flimsy birch sapling that snapped in two as he hauled himself to his feet again. His thigh burned, lancing pain that shot upward into his groin so that he moaned.

God, I hope I'm not too late, please don't let it be too late.

Overhead the moon broke free of the trees, shone down upon the winding sliver of road and, to one side, the small clearing where a lone Jaguar was parked. In the distance, the lights of the Goines mansion showed fitfully through a scrim of brush and overgrown yew. He could hear voices calling faintly, the plaintive cry of a barn owl. Panting, he ran into the clearing, his feet thudding more softly now on packed leaves and earth.

At sight of the car he slowed. What with the screaming pain in his leg, the fire in his chest from running, he hadn't thought that anything else could hurt him, but he was wrong. The Jag was utterly still: no muted screams, no stifled voice, nothing. He approached it as though it were a bomb, his hands clenched at his sides, then stopped and ran his fingers over the trunk, feeling where he had punched several holes with a tire iron. Finally he dug the key from his pocket and with trembling fingers pushed it into the lock.

The trunk swung open. Moonlight picked out a crumpled form, like a heap of old clothing wadded in the narrow space. Suddenly the heap moved. Cole caught a glint of jewelry, Kathryn's wristwatch, the thick mat of dark hair as she scrambled from the trunk, her eyes brimming with tears of rage.

"You bastard! You *total bastard!*"

He backed away as she lunged drunkenly for him, arms swinging wildly. His leg buckled and he slipped and fell onto the leaf-strewn ground. With a cry Kathryn began kicking him, shouting hysterically.

"I could have *died* in there! If something had happened to you, I would have *died!*"

He looked up at her, helpless, his lip caked with blood. "I—I—I'm really sorry," he said weakly.

Kathryn's leg swung wildly, missing Cole and sending her off balance. She caught herself, breathing hard, and glared down at him, her tangled hair a shadowy halo about her livid face. For the first time she noticed his torn and filthy clothes, the spattering of blood across his face and arms.

"What have you done?" she asked hoarsely. She drew a hand to her mouth. "Did you—kill someone?"

"No!" Cole cried. He pushed himself up and struggled to his feet. "I—I don't think so." He stared at her, his face a twisted mask of anguish and horror. "I mean—maybe I killed millions of people! *Billions!*"

Kathryn rubbed her pounding forehead and cast a quick grateful glance at the moon overhead. "What?" she asked more calmly.

"I—I'm sorry I locked you up." Cole continued to gaze at her with huge eyes. "I came back, I put some holes in the trunk so you could breathe." His eyes grew unfocused and he shook his head, as though an insect were bothering him. "I thought—I thought—Do you think I might be crazy?"

Kathryn stared at him. She felt her fear and rage fall away, her professional detachment rising like a shield. She nodded, very slowly.

"What made you think that, James?" she asked in a soothing voice.

Cole's balled fists drummed nervously at his sides. He lifted his face and stared blankly at the moonlit sky. "Jeffrey Goines said it was *my* idea about the virus. And suddenly, I wasn't sure. We talked about it when I was in the institution, and it was all . . . fuzzy. The drugs and stuff . . . "

Abruptly he looked right at her, his fists bunched

before his chest. "You think maybe *I'm* the one who wiped out the human race? It was *my* idea?"

Kathryn shook her head, smiling gently. She was in control again. "Nobody is going to wipe out the human race. Not you or Jeffrey or anybody else. You've created something in your mind, James—a substitute reality—in order to avoid something you don't want to face."

James nodded. Unbidden the image came into his mind of the airport, a blurred figure falling to the ground; something terrible he had seen, something—

The image was gone. Cole blinked. "I'm . . . 'mentally divergent,'" he said, remembering L. J. Washington's term. "I would love to believe that."

Kathryn nodded. "It can be dealt with, but only if you want to. I can help you, James," she added softly.

From somewhere in the near distance echoed the sound of voices in the woods, barking dogs. Cole's gaze darted to where the road could be glimpsed at the edge of the clearing. "I need help all right. They're after me! Chasing me!"

"Who, James? Who is after you?"

He gestured in the direction of the noise. "I think—I think some of the people at the party were—policemen!"

"Party?" Kathryn looked at him in disbelief. "You went to a—"

She ran a hand through her hair, grimacing. "Never mind. If that *is* the police, it's important that you *surrender* to them, instead of them catching you running. Okay?"

Cole nodded, only half hearing her. Suddenly he

brightened. "It would be great if I'm crazy. If I'm wrong about everything then the world will be okay. I'll never have to live underground."

A hound bayed unnervingly nearby. Kathryn glanced into the woods. Flashlights played against the bare trees, touched on a boulder only a hundred feet away. She took a deep breath. "Give me the gun."

"The gun!" Cole opened his hands, stared at them in dismay. "I lost it."

Relief flooded Kathryn. "You're sure?"

Cole nodded. He tilted his head back, gazing up at the glowing moon, the stars flung like handfuls of snow across the velvety sky. "Stars! Air!" he whispered reverently. "I can live here! Breathe!"

For a moment Kathryn watched him: a grown man, a psychotic ex-con in torn and bloodstained clothes, staring at the sky like a child on Christmas Eve. A sharp sad sense of loss swept through her, but she pushed it aside.

It's better this way, she thought. *It has to be better. . . .*

She started around to the front of the car. "I'm going to attract their attention, let them know where we are, okay, James?" She got into the driver's seat and honked the horn—once, twice, again. A volley of frenzied yelps came in reply. "They'll tell you to put your hands on top of your head," she went on briskly. "Do what they tell you. You're going to get better, James—I know it!"

Cole said nothing. He raised his arms to the sky, an instant later let them fall. He looked down at the ground at his feet, saw something poking up through the dead leaves. Awkwardly, trying not to put too much weight on his bad leg, he lowered himself, reaching tentatively for the pale blade that thrust up amongst twigs and oak mast. Moonlight drifted through the trees to touch a crocus, its tiny leaves peeling back to reveal the flower's small bright heart. With heartbreaking gentleness Cole touched the blossom, its cool, slightly damp pressure like a tiny mouth meeting his finger. With a low moan his hands closed around dead leaves, brought them to his face and rubbed them over his cheeks. He inhaled their sweet must, opened his lips so that crumbled bits of leaf and earth and bark fell into his mouth, and swallowed them, half-mad with joy. As the Jag's horn blared, he gazed up at the sky, the full moon and stars and trees and all the glory of it: this breathless wonder, this dream he had somehow awakened into. He began to weep, tears running down his face and mingling with the fragments of tree and leaf.

"I love this world!"

From the woods came a sudden shout. Cole stared rapturously at the sky as Kathryn hurried out of the car and started toward him.

"Remember, I'm going to help you," she said. "I'll stay with you. I won't let them—"

She broke off in mid-sentence, staring stunned as policemen and yelping dogs raced into the clearing.

Cole was gone. Where he had been there was only a small mound of disturbed leaves, and the fragile finger of a yellow crocus thrusting from the earth.

†

They kept her all night at the station house. Periodically the faces around her changed, from the local police detectives to FBI agents to a kind-faced staffer who brought her coffee and, later, a small carton of orange juice.

Now, with early morning sunlight slanting in through windows gray with steel mesh and dead flies, the exhausted Kathryn found herself telling her story for the fifth time. Her listener was Lieutenant Halperin, a man approaching retirement whose lined face showed signs of not being able to wait for it much longer.

". . . Then I said something to him about cooperating and he said he would do that, so I got in the car and started honking the horn. When I got out, he was gone."

Halperin took a sip of his coffee, nodding. Behind him another cop entered the room and handed him an 8x10 photo.

"You lucked out," Halperin said, his eyes darting from the photo to the bedraggled woman sitting across from him. She'd combed her hair and washed up, but her clothes were rumpled and stained, her face haggard from her ordeal. "For a while we thought you were a body they found downstate—mutilated."

Kathryn shook her head resolutely. "He wouldn't do something like that. He—"

Lieutenant Halperin interrupted her. "This the man he attacked?"

He handed Kathryn the photo. She stared at it, a gritty black-and-white showing one of the men who'd attacked them in the crackhouse in Philadelphia. He was slumped against the alley wall, his head drooping at an unnatural angle against his shoulder. Kathryn gave a quick nod and pushed the photo back across the table.

"I'd like to be clear about this," she said firmly. *"That* man—" she stabbed at the photo "—and the other one, were . . . *severely* beating us. James Cole didn't start it. He *saved* me."

Halperin leaned back in his chair, sighing. "Funny thing, Doctor—maybe you can explain it to me, you being a psychiatrist. Why do kidnap victims almost always try to tell us about the guys who grabbed 'em and try to make us understand how *kind* these bastards really were?"

"It's a normal reaction to a life-threatening situation," she replied in a monotone. Suddenly her eyes brightened, and she looked directly at Halperin. "He's *sick*. He thinks he comes from the future. He's been living in a carefully constructed fantasy world and that world is starting to disintegrate. He needs *help!*"

"Help," Halperin repeated. His fingers drummed slowly at the table edge. After a moment he shook his head, gathering his notes and the photo. "Well. I'm sure we'll do all we can to *help* this guy. Dr. Railly—"

He stood and motioned her to the door. "There's a little more paperwork for you to finish, and then someone will help you make arrangements to get back home."

"Thank you," Kathryn said in a small voice, her

burst of excitement played out. "Thank you very much."

And she followed him out the door.

Voices drown the roar of a jet, the lingering echo of a gunshot. Near the boy's feet two blond heads lean together, their bright hair tangling, the woman cradling the wounded man where he sprawls on the concourse. Despite his terror the boy wants to dart forward, to join them, but someone holds him back, there is a hand on his shoulder, a voice commanding him.

"Wake up! Wake up!"

He flinched as a second voice chimed in. "I think we gave him too much."

"WAKE UP, PRISONER!"

He woke, blinking as he tried to focus on the blurry faces hovering over him.

"Come on, Cole, cooperate!"

"Spit it out! You went to the home of a famous virologist . . ."

With great effort Cole shook his head. "You—don't exist!" he finally said, the words like stones falling from his mouth. "You're only in—my mind . . ."

Above him the blur coalesced into a single face: the microbiologist, his sunglasses a heavy bar above his thin mouth. "Speak up, Cole," he ordered. "What did you do next?"

Cole closed his eyes, forced those other faces from his mind. Instead he tried to bring up the image of a moonlit sky, the shadow of a crocus leaf upon his outstretched palm, Kathryn Railly's pale eyes and determined frown as she gently pulled gauze across his leg.

"Cole!"

The images grew clearer. He could hear dead leaves rustling, the faint sigh of wind in the trees. He smiled, feeling the wind on his shorn scalp, then cried aloud as cold fingers pressed down upon his shoulder, probed at his neck until they found a vein. There was the sudden stab of a needle, then darkness.

In Kathryn's apartment, her friends Marilou and Wayne sat huddled together on the couch, riveted by the TV. A film clip showed a fragile-looking Kathryn leaving the police station, her face dead white, her hair hidden by a scarf.

"Exhausted, but apparently unharmed by her thirty-hour ordeal, Dr. Railly returned to Baltimore this morning without making a public statement."

Behind them the bedroom door opened. Wayne fumbled hastily with the remote, turning down the volume as Kathryn crossed the room in her bathrobe, her cat cradled in her arms. Wayne looked up at her, crestfallen.

"Sorry. Did we wake you?"

Kathryn shook her head. "No. I'm too hyped up to sleep."

Marilou moved over to make room for her on the couch. "Did you take the sedative?"

"God no. I hate those things. They mess my head up." She took the remote from Wayne's hand and turned the volume back up.

"*Along with the kidnapping of the Baltimore woman, James Cole is now also wanted in connection with the brutal slaying of Rodney Wiggins, an ex-convict from . . .*"

With a sigh, Kathryn crossed the room to the window. She pushed aside the drape, looked down to see a beaten-up old Ford parked on the other side of the street. Inside sat a man wearing sunglasses, his face tilted up toward her window: Detective Dalva, Baltimore PD.

"These damn cops," Kathryn said to no one in particular. "I told them and told them do they really expect him to come here?" She turned and started for the little kitchen. Marilou followed her, helping her get tea things out.

"*And in Fresno, California . . .*"

Kathryn glanced sadly back at the TV. "He's dead, isn't he—that little boy?"

Wayne rolled his eyes. "He's fine. It was just a prank he and his friends pulled."

Kathryn's shocked gaze remained fixed on the TV, where a sheepish young boy was being led out of a barn by police.

"*. . . and authorities have so far been noncommittal about whether they will try to file charges against the families of the children involved in the hoax.*"

"Kathryn! What is it?" Marilou's worried face peered over her friend's shoulder. "Are you—"

Kathryn shook her head. Her hands felt numb; her entire body felt as though it had been drenched in icy spray. She shook her head, still staring in growing fear at the television. She fought to keep her voice steady as she replied.

"A mistake . . . I think there's been . . . a very, very, bad mistake."

Trees, a sky bluer than any he has ever seen. A softness upon his face that Cole at first thinks is snow, but instead is Kathryn Railly's hair, her mouth grazing his. He groans with pleasure, smiles as he hears someone singing in a low voice—

"I found my thri—ill
On Blueberry Hill . . . "

The voice grows louder, becomes several voices, many voices, singing raggedly now.

". . . on Blueberry Hill . . . "

His hand gropes at his face, finds nothing there. The off-key singing continues, louder and more robust. When he opened his eyes, there was no sky, no trees, no Kathryn. Only a ring of earnest scientists crowded around Cole's bed, belting out a barely listenable tune.

"Huh?" Cole shook his head.

Seeing that he was awake, the scientists broke off singing and burst into applause.

"Well done, James!"

"Nice going! Good for you!"

"Congratulations!"

Cole sat up, confused. The kind-eyed zoologist leaned over him, running a hand across his brow.

"During your 'interview,' while you were under the influence, you told us you liked music!" she explained happily.

Cole drew away from her and looked around. He was in a small windowless room, his narrow iron cot the only furniture. The stained white walls were adorned with cheap cardboard reproductions of nine-teenth-century landscape paintings, trees and hillsides tinted in cheerless shades of green and brown. When he tried to lift his hands, he found that they were very loosely attached with white ribbons to his bed.

The zoologist moved closer, reacting to his disbe-lief with a disarming smile. "This isn't the prison, James," she said soothingly. "This is a hospital."

"But just until you recover your equilibrium," interrupted the microbiologist, grinning beneath his black glasses. "You're still a little—disoriented."

"Stress!" agreed the astrophysicist. He pushed a shock of silvery hair from his forehead. "Time travel!"

The microbiologist nodded sagely. "You stood up very well, considering."

"Superior work!" cried the zoologist. "Superior!" She sat on the edge of Cole's bed, heedless of his dis-may and unease. "You connected the Army of the Twelve Monkeys to a world-famous virologist and his son—"

"Others will take over now," the microbiologist said officiously. "We'll be back on the surface in a couple of months."

The others broke in excitedly.

"We'll retake the planet."

"We're very close!"

"Because of *you!*"

The microbiologist stepped forward, unrolling a document. "This is it, James—what you've been waiting for."

Cole eyed it warily. "A full pardon!" cried the zoologist.

"You'll be out of here in no time," the microbiologist added, clapping a hand on Cole's shoulder. "Women will want to get to know you—"

Shouting, Cole pulled himself free. "I don't want your women! *I want to be well!*"

Two guards Cole hadn't seen until now burst through the little circle and pushed Cole onto the bed.

"Of course you want to be well, James," the microbiologist said, looking on approvingly as the guards tightened the restraints around Cole's wrists. "And you will be—soon."

"YOU DON'T EXIST!" yelled Cole. He kicked at the microbiologist, sent his pardon flying. "*YOU'RE NOT REAL!* HA HA HA! PEOPLE DON'T TRAVEL IN TIME! YOU AREN'T HERE! I MADE YOU UP! YOU CAN'T TRICK ME! YOU'RE IN MY MIND! I'M INSANE AND *YOU'RE MY INSANITY!*"

Hysterical laughter filled the room as the scientists backed toward the door. "YOU CAN'T TRICK ME!" shrieked Cole. "NOT ANYMORE!"

"I think Mr. Cole is tired," the microbiologist said pointedly to one of the guards. "I think perhaps we need to help him sleep again."

Nodding, the guard held up a needle and began to

struggle with Cole until he had him pinioned to the bed.

"There," the microbiologist murmured, standing alone in the doorway. "That's better. We don't blame you for getting excited, James—pardons don't come every day. But now, I think it would be best for you to rest now—rest for just as long as you can."

Kathryn had Dr. Fletcher cornered in his office. The chief of psychiatry looked distinctly uncomfortable in his swivel chair. He removed his tinted glasses, wiped them with a tissue, replaced them on his nose, then a moment later performed the whole little ritual all over again.

"He not only used the word 'prank,' he said the boy was hiding in the barn," Kathryn said intensely.

Fletcher nodded, began tapping his pen on his desk. "He *kidnapped* you, Kathryn," he said when she paused for breath. "You saw him murder someone. You knew there was a real possibility he would kill you, too. You were under tremendous emotional stress."

"For God's sake, Owen, *listen to me*—he knew about the boy in Fresno and he says five billion people are going to die!"

Fletcher sighed. He held his pencil in both hands, staring fixedly at her. He'd seen patients like this before, even one or two residents, but never someone on his staff. Certainly not someone who, until recently, he had perceived to be as level-headed as Kathryn Railly. After a moment he leaned forward, hands extended imploringly.

"Kathryn, you *know* he can't possibly know that. You're a rational person. You're a trained psychiatrist. *You* know the difference between what's real and what's not."

"And what we believe is what's accepted as truth now, isn't it, Owen?" Kathryn exploded. "Psychiatry—it's the latest religion! And *we're* the priests—we decide what's right and what's wrong. *We* decide who's crazy and who isn't."

She whirled and started for the door, stopped and cast one last look back at Fletcher where he sat, his degrees and awards and citations glowing on the wall behind him like so many little windows. "Well, you know what, Owen?" she said, her voice low and shaking. "I'm in trouble. I'm losing my faith."

Dr. Fletcher sighed again as the door slammed behind her.

Alone in his room, Cole twisted on the bed, trying to free himself from his restraints. Whatever drug they had given him had worn off and left him feeling murderous. He could almost bring one tied wrist over the bedrail, where a rusted hinge rose like a jagged tooth. If he could reach that he might be able to saw the restraint in two, and then . . .

"You sure fucked up, Bob!"

Cole grew rigid. He glanced quickly around the empty room, the sad excuses for art on the filthy walls, then once more moved his arm against the rusted bedrail.

"But I can understand you don't want your mistakes

pointed out to you," the hoarse voice went on gleefully. "I can relate to that, old Bob."

In spite of himself, Cole hesitated and looked around again. The room was empty.

"Hey, I know what you're thinking," the voice rasped. "You're thinking I don't exist except in your head. I can see that point of view. But you could still talk to me, couldn't you? Carry on a decent conversation."

Cole's eyes widened. "I saw you!" he cried. "In the real world! You pulled out your teeth."

"Why would I pull out my teeth, Bob?" the voice chastened him. "They don't like that. That's a no-no. And when did you say you saw me—in 1872?"

The voice cackled as Cole screamed, "FUCK YOU!"

"Yelling won't get you what you want. You have to be smart to get what you want."

"Oh, yeah?" panted Cole. "What do I want?"

"You don't know what you want? Sure you do, Bob. You know what you want."

"Tell me," cried Cole. He rocked back and forth on the metal bed. "Tell me what I want."

Silence. Then, in a suggestive tone, the voice answered.

"To see the sky—and the ocean. To be topside. Breathe the air. To be with her. Isn't that right? Isn't that what you want?"

Utterly shaken, Cole held his breath for a long moment. When he finally spoke, he could scarcely hear his own words.

"More . . . than . . . anything," he whispered.

✝

That night Kathryn slept fitfully, her dreams all of struggle and flight, the horizon filled with burning clouds and the figure of a muscular man, hair shorn and face bloodied, fleeing across a ravaged landscape. When the phone rang she sat up with a gasp, immediately wide awake.

"Hello?"

"Dr. Railly? Jim Halperin, Philly PD. Sorry to call so early but—"

She clutched the phone eagerly to her face. "You found him? Is he all right?"

A beat. Then, *"Au contraire,* Doctor. No sign of your good friend the kidnapper. However, the plot thickens. I have a report on my desk that says the bullet you claim you removed from Mr. Cole's thigh is an antique, and . . ."

Halperin paused. Kathryn's heart began to thump dangerously fast. ". . . and all indications are it was fired sometime prior to 1920."

Kathryn stiffened, stared at her rumpled bed.

"So what I was thinking, Dr. Railly, was how 'bout I take a little spin down there and maybe we could have a bite to eat and maybe you might wanna revise or amplify your statement . . . Hello? Hello? Dr. Railly?"

Kathryn held the phone at arm's length, still gazing at it in horror, then very slowly replaced it in the cradle. She sat for a minute, trying to slow her racing heart, then abruptly stood and hurried into her study. She went to the bookcase that held all of her research for *The Doomsday Syndrome* and frantically began pulling down the neatly arranged piles of papers and books, throwing them across the floor. Finally she found what she was searching for: a manila folder crammed with old photographs. With shaking hands she rummaged through it, spilling negatives and faded 8x10s, until her fingers closed on a sepia-toned print.

"*No!*"

The room's silence shattered as she held up the photograph, an uncropped shot of a young Latino man being carried on a stretcher through the trenches of World War I France. In the corner of the photo, with no helmet, no gas mask, and just a bit of bare shoulder showing, crouched James Cole.

In the scientists' conference room, Cole met his masters: the microbiologist with the hidden eyes; the zoologist, even now staring at him with pity, her hands neatly clasped in her lap; the earnest silver-haired astrophysicist, nervously tugging his single gold earring. At the far end of the conference table were the other scientists, silent and grim. Cole stood in front of them all, clean-shaven, clear-eyed, gazing unabashed into the microbiologist's scowling face.

"The food, the sky, the certain, uh—sexual temptations—" The microbiologist tapped his pencil against one finger. "You haven't become addicted, have you, Cole? To that dying world?"

Cole shook his head. His mouth was dry; he could already feel sweat trickling down his neck, but his voice was steady as he replied.

"No, sir! I just want to do my part. To get us back on top *in charge* of the planet. And I have the experience, I know who the people are—"

"He really *is* the most qualified," the zoologist said softly.

The microbiologist leaned back in his rickety chair, tilting his head so that his black glasses caught the light. "But all that—*behavior.*"

The astrophysicist nodded. "You said we weren't *real*, Cole." He sounded a little hurt.

Cole thrust his shoulders back. "Well, sir, I don't think the human mind was built to exist in two different—whatever you call it—dimensions. It's stressful. You said it yourselves: it gets you confused. You don't know what's real and what's not."

Behind his dark glasses, the microbiologist's expression was unreadable. "But you know what's real now?"

"Yes, sir."

"You can't trick us, you know. It wouldn't work."

"No, sir. I mean, yes, I understand that. I want to help."

The three scientists looked at each other, then at Cole. After a moment the microbiologist stood and walked over to the wall covered with fading photos and torn newspaper clippings. In the middle of these a worn, much-creased map of the world was held in place with tacks and curling tape.

"Let's consider again our current information," he began, using his pencil as a pointer to indicate various spots on the map. "If the symptoms were first detected in Philadelphia on December 27, 1996, that makes us know that . . ." He turned questioningly to Cole.

"That it was released in Philadelphia, probably on December 13, 1996."

The microbiologist allowed himself a small nod of approbation. "And it appeared sequentially after that in?"

Cole shot a quick glance at the others staring at him from the long table, then answered in the dutiful tones of a prize student.

"San Francisco, New Orleans, Rio de Janeiro, Rome, Kinshasa, Karachi, Bangkok, then Peking."

The microbiologist raised an eyebrow. "Meaning?"

"That the virus was taken from Philadelphia to San Francisco, then to New Orleans, Rio de Janeiro, Rome, Kinshasa, Karachi, Bangkok, then Peking."

"And your *only* goal is . . . ?"

"To find out where the virus is so a qualified scientist can travel back into the past and study the original virus."

"So that?"

Cole frowned. "Uh, so that a vaccine can be developed that will, uh, allow mankind to reclaim the surface of the earth."

Murmurs as the scientists turned to each other, nodding as they assessed Cole's performance. Cole allowed himself a small sigh of relief, then let his eyes drift across the melange of clues spread across the walls: magazine covers, newspapers, obituaries, charts. Among them was an 8x10 photo of graffiti on a wall, crudely painted letters that spelled out an urgent message.

ATTENTION! POLICE ARE WATCHING!
IS THERE A VIRUS? IS THIS THE SOURCE?
5,000,000,000 DIE?

His gaze lingered on the photo, trying to figure if he recognized it, when he heard a voice saying, "Cole—Mr. Cole—"

He turned and saw the silver-haired astrophysicist, his earnest face creased by a smile repeated in the faces of the other scientists who were now crowding around him.

"That was very well done, Cole. *Very* well done."

Standing in front of a glass wall in his office, Leland Goines paced angrily back and forth, cordless phone to his ear. The wall overlooked a vast sterile lab where workers in white, hooded suits, like astronauts or surreal ghosts, scurried among stainless steel vats and freezers, peering into cages and withdrawing tubes and bottles and trays. In the office behind him, Goines' assistant, a man in black T-shirt and jeans, his lank red hair pulled back into a ponytail, flipped idly through the latest issue of *Lancet*.

"You have reason to believe my son may be planning to do *what?*"

Goines waited impatiently as the woman on the other end of the telephone went on, "Yes, I *do* understand, Dr. Goines, I *know* it sounds insane but—"

Goines waved a hand dismissively and broke in. "I'm afraid this doesn't seem very professional to me,

Dr. Railly. In fact, it's distressingly *un*professional! I don't know anything about 'monkey armies,' Doctor. Nothing whatsoever. If my son ever was involved in—"

He paused, then went on angrily. "Well, it would be doubly inappropriate to discuss matters of security with you, Dr. Railly, but if it will put you at ease, neither my son nor any other unauthorized person has access to any potentially dangerous organisms in this laboratory. Thank you for your concern."

He slammed the phone down and glared across the room at his assistant. Seeing Goines' expression, the red-haired man tossed the magazine aside and stood.

"Dr. *Kathryn* Railly?" he asked casually.

Goines nodded and raised his hands in exasperation. "The psychiatrist who was kidnapped by that man who broke into my house. She seems to have been suddenly struck by the most preposterous notion about Jeffrey."

His assistant rolled his eyes. "I attended a lecture of hers once. Apocalyptic visions." He stretched and walked over to a coat rack, took down a white lab jacket with DR. PETERS embroidered on the pocket. "Has she succumbed to her own theoretical 'Cassandra Complex'?"

But Leland Goines stood lost in thought at the glass wall, staring down at the white-suited lab workers in their glass-and-steel city. "Given the nature of our work, we can't ever be careful enough," he said at last. "I think we should review our security procedures, perhaps upgrade them."

At the door Dr. Peters stopped, nodding obediently,

and waited for further instructions. When there were none, he said, "Of course. I'll notify Hudson and Drake immediately."

"Thank you," Dr. Goines said absently. Long after Peters was gone he remained where he stood, his face impassive as he gazed at his kingdom below.

Inside Iacono's abandoned butcher shop, five nervous animal activists crouched motionless amidst cardboard cartons and toppled stacks of brochures. After a few minutes Fale took a deep breath, pushed a strand of pale hair from his pale face, then scuttled across the floor to the front window. He pressed his eye to a slit between posters and peered outside.

"Who is it?" whispered Bee.

Fale shook his head in disbelief. "It's that kidnap woman—the one who was with the guy who tied us up."

"What's she doing?"

"She's drawing attention to us, that's what she's doing!" Fale glared over his shoulder. "I don't know what you're up to this time, Goines, but you're gonna get us in deep shit!"

Jeffrey Goines yawned and leaned back, pillowing his head on a stack of MEAT IS MURDER flyers. "Whine, whine, whine. What about walkie-talkies? We *used* to have walkie-talkies."

Fale and the rest looked at each other blankly.

"Well?" demanded Jeffrey. "*Didn't* we?"

Outside, Kathryn Railly pounded futilely at the door. Further down the littered sidewalk, several derelicts watched with interest as she furiously stalked back and forth.

"I know you're in there!" she yelled, rattling the handle for the hundredth time. "I saw you! I saw someone moving!"

"Secret experiments!" someone whispered in a hoarse voice.

Kathryn whirled, fists drawn defensively to her chest. In front of her stood the same toothless street person she had seen there days before.

"That's what they do!" he explained triumphantly. *"Secret weird stuff!"*

"You! I know you!"

The bum shuffled past her, studying the pictures of tortured animals on the storefront. "Not just on 'em," he said thoughtfully, poking at one poster with a scabby finger. "Do 'em on people, too—down at the shelters. I *know*," he added in a conspiratorial aside. "Feed 'em chemicals and take pictures of 'em."

Kathryn nodded her head quickly, agreeing with him. "Have you seen James Cole? The man who—"

"They're watchin' you," the bum whispered. His eyes moved toward the street. "Takin' pictures."

Kathryn followed his look. Across the street, beside an overflowing trash can, was parked the familiar old Ford with Detective Dalva slouched behind the wheel, pretending to read a newspaper.

"The police. I know." Kathryn brushed her hair from her eyes and took a step toward the derelict. "Listen, I need to talk to James, but he has to be careful how he contacts me. He mustn't get caught. Do you understand me?"

The weather-beaten man eyed her warily through red-rimmed eyes. "Uh, yeah, sure. Who's James?"

"He was with me, he spoke to you," said Kathryn, her voice growing more agitated. "Several weeks ago. He said you were from the future—watching him."

The man sucked his cheeks in, eyebrows raised, and started to back away from her. "Uh, I don't think so," he said nervously. "I think maybe you got the wrong—"

Just then, two skinhead boys on skateboards slammed around the corner, tagging their way along the filthy sidewalk with cans of spray paint. Kathryn watched, then without a word raced toward them. The derelict turned and fled.

At the window of the Freedom for Animals Association headquarters, one intense brown eye blinked, then turned away.

"You get the bolt cutters?" called Jeffrey, reading from a checklist.

"One dozen. They're in the van," answered Teddy.

"Hey!" Bee excitedly beckoned the others to the window. "Do you know what she's doing?"

Teddy and Fale hurried to the window and peered out. Barely three feet away stood Kathryn Railly, spray-painting the front of the store.

"What's it say?" wondered Teddy.

Bee shook her head. "I can't see it."

Jeffrey slammed down his checklist and shouted, "WHY DON'T WE *FORGET* MY GODDAMN PSYCHIATRIST AND DEAL WITH THE TASK AT HAND! *THIS* IS IMPORTANT!"

Fale spun around. "*Your* psychiatrist? Did you just say, *your* psychiatrist?"

Jeffrey looked at him balefully and retrieved his list. "*Ex*-psychiatrist! Now, what about flashlights? How many flashlights?"

Fale shook his head, pointing at the window. "That woman is—was—your psychiatrist? And now she's spray-painting our building?"

Jeffrey shrugged. "Rent a fucking life, Fale. And while you're at it, find our goddamn flashlights."

On the sidewalk, Kathryn darted back and forth, shaking and waving the can of spray paint as she wrote in sweeping letters across the walled-up storefront. A small crowd of street people inched up behind her, their amazement mirrored by that of Detective Dalva in his old Ford.

"I don't fucking believe this," he murmured. He grabbed his clipboard and scribbled something on a sheet of paper, never moving his eyes from Kathryn. "She really *is* a fruitcake."

A white-haired drunk swayed beside Kathryn, pronouncing each letter aloud. The two punks who'd sold her the spray paint buzzed past on their boards, shouting derisively. She never glanced back, just continued like a woman possessed, heedless of black paint spattering her clothes and face. And so she didn't see the newcomer shambling through the knot of onlookers, a broad-shouldered white man in shabby clothes and close-cropped hair, blinking as though the feeble winter sunlight hurt his eyes. When he was a few feet away from Kathryn he stopped, shading his eyes with his hands, and stared at her in astonishment.

"Kathryn!"

She whipped around, the crowd scattering as flecks of paint sprayed across them.

"James!"

He started toward her, arms outstretched piteously. But before he reached her, Kathryn looked past him to where Detective Dalva sat watching the two of them with renewed interest.

"James!" she hissed urgently, cocking a thumb at the worn-out car. "That's a policeman! Pretend you don't know me. If he sees you . . ."

"No." Cole turned and stared directly at the car. "I *want* to turn myself in! Where is he?"

He placed his hands on his head and gave Kathryn an earnest look. "Don't worry—it's all okay now. I'm not crazy anymore! I mean, I *am* crazy, mentally divergent actually, but I *know* it now, and I want *you* to help me. I want to get well."

Kathryn grabbed his hands, trying desperately to pull them from his head as she sought to block the detective's view of Cole.

"James! Put your hands down and *listen* to me. Things have changed!" She glanced back frantically at the car, saw Dalva reach for his clipboard and hold up a photograph. He checked the image against Cole standing on the sidewalk, then reached for his radio mike. Kathryn fought back a cry, tossed aside her spray can and grabbed Cole, trying to pull him after her.

"James, come on! We have to get out of here *now*—"

But Cole didn't move. Instead he looked from the

spray can rolling on the sidewalk to the wall that
Railly had painted. Shaky black letters covered plywood and taped-up glass and old brick.

ATTENTION! POLICE ARE WATCHING!
IS THERE A VIRUS? IS THIS THE SOURCE?
5,000,000,000 DIE?

"I've—I've seen that before," he whispered.

Kathryn shook her head. "James, trust me. We're
in terrible trouble. We have to run—"

She dragged him along the sidewalk past several
bemused onlookers. Cole's eyes remained fixed on
the wall, but Kathryn stumbled along like a mad-
woman, her hair disheveled, black paint flecked on
her clothes. As they turned the corner, the Ford suddenly shot from its space. It made a sharp U-turn,
nearly colliding with a passing delivery van in a harsh
squeal of brakes and blaring horns.

Inside the storefront, Fale stood behind Bee,
frowning. "*Now* what's happening?" he demanded.

Bee shook her head in amazement. "Wow. Some
guy in a Ford is chasing her and some other guy I
can't see."

From outside came shouted curses and another
peal of brakes. Turning from the window, Fale threw
up his hands in disgust.

"Hey, *no problem!*" he cried. "It's probably just
another kidnapping featuring Jeffrey's *shrink*, pardon
me, make that *ex*-shrink—"

The others stopped what they were doing to look
up at him, standing now in the middle of the room

and pointing at Jeffrey. "*This* is your leader," yelled Fale, "a certifiable lunatic who told his former *psychiatrist* all his plans for God knows what wacko irresponsible schemes, and now who knows what she's painted out there *on our wall?*"

Jeffrey crossed the room to Fale and jabbed him in the stomach with his finger. "WHO CARES WHAT PSYCHIATRISTS WRITE ON WALLS?" Bee and Teddy backed away as he went on, "You think I told her about the Army of the Twelve Monkeys? Impossible! Know why, you pathetically ineffectual and pusillanimous pretend-friend-to-animals? I'll tell you why—because when I had anything to do with her *six years ago*, there was no such thing—*I hadn't even thought of it yet!*"

"Oh, yeah?" Fale shouted back triumphantly. "Then how come she knows what's going on?"

Jeffrey tossed his head back. His rage suddenly melted into supercilious good humor.

"Here's my theory on that," he said in a patronizing tone. "While I was institutionalized, my brain was studied exhaustively in the guise of mental health. I was interrogated, X-rayed, examined thoroughly. Then, everything about me was entered into a computer where they created a *model* of my *mind.*"

The others watched, mesmerized, as Jeffrey preened and gestured grandly. "*Then,*" he continued, "using the computer model, they generated every thought I could possibly have in the next, say, ten years, which they *then* filtered through a probability matrix to determine everything I was going to do in that period."

He paused, beaming condescendingly at his audience. "So you see, she *knew* I was going to lead the Army of the Twelve Monkeys in the pages of history before it ever even *occurred* to me. She knows everything I'm ever *going* to do before I know it myself. How about that?"

He smiled smugly at the flabbergasted Fale, then fastidiously bent to pick up a stray flyer. "Now I have to get going," he ended lightly. "Do my part. You guys check all this stuff out and load up the van. Make sure you get everything," he called back in a singsong voice as he paraded to the back door. "I'm outta here."

Fale and Teddy and Bee stared after him, watching the door slam closed. When Jeffrey's footsteps finally died away, Fale turned to the others, his eyes wide.

"He's seriously crazy. You know that."

"Oh, duh," said Bee. She gave Fale a disgusted look, then followed Jeffrey through the back room.

Several blocks away, Kathryn Railly and James Cole crouched in a heap of garbage, their heads covered with the remains of a cardboard box. Behind them loomed a once-lovely art nouveau building, its ornate facade now slashed with graffiti and shattered windows. At the base of the building spread a squalid cardboard shantytown, men and women and children huddled behind bits of broken plywood, or warming themselves by a small bonfire.

"Shh!" Kathryn whispered as Cole moved slightly beneath their protection, sending a shower of crumbled safety glass onto their heads. A few yards away, Detective Dalva's unmarked Ford crawled slowly down the desolate alley. Behind its windshield she could clearly see Dalva's eyes, carefully scrutinizing each rusted garbage can, every suspicious face peering at him from their pathetic hovels. After an interminable time, the car passed from view, disappearing into the next burnt-out city block. Gasping, Kathryn scrambled from the refuse, ignoring the glares of the shantytown residents.

"James! Come on——"

Shaking his head in confusion, Cole crawled out after her. He brushed sawdust from his hair, then said, "I don't understand what we're doing, Kathryn."

Kathryn looked around uneasily. "We're avoiding the police until I can——talk to you."

Cole's eyes lit up. "You mean, treat me? Cure me?"

Almost immediately the hope drained from him. He stared back down the way they'd come and said in a lower voice, "Kathryn——those words on the wall back there——I've seen them before. I——I dreamed them. When I was sick."

Kathryn stopped and stared at him. "I——I know," she said at last. She shivered, pulling her jacket closed and for the first time noticing James' thin cotton shirt and faded trousers. Her tone grew soft. "James——you must be freezing. Here——"

She looked around, her eyes falling on a rundown skid row hotel across the street. Broken plastic letters spelled out: THE GLOBE: ROOMS WEEKLY, DAILY.

"Come on," she said, taking James by the hand and leading him to the door.

Inside, an ancient hotel clerk with tremulous hands and a vulture's glassy stare eyed them suspiciously from behind a cracked Formica counter.

"Thirty-five bucks an hour," he wheezed.

Kathryn looked at him in disbelief. "An *hour?*"

The clerk scowled. "You want quarter hours, go someplace else."

Just then, a dazed-looking woman teetered down the stairs, resplendent in a beaded wig, platform shoes, and rubber dress. James watched her curiously, but Kathryn quickly turned away and began counting out bills.

"Here's twenty, twenty-five, twenty-seven." She held up the last dollar bill and gazed coldly at the clerk. "For one hour. Deal?"

The clerk squinted warily at the money, finally scooped it and turned to get a key.

"One hour, honey-babe." He looked Kathryn up and down, taking in her soiled clothes, the bits of paper and sawdust still clinging to her hair. He grimaced. "Number forty-four. Fourth floor. Up the stairs, enda the hall. Elevator's busted."

As Kathryn grabbed the key and turned, Cole leaned across the Formica counter and hissed, "She's not 'honey-babe.' She's a *doctor.* She's my psychiatrist. You got that?" Cole pounded the counter, then followed Kathryn upstairs.

"Whatever gets it up for you, Jack," the clerk muttered when Cole was safely out of earshot. He waited until the two disappeared upstairs. Then, making faces and mumbling to himself, he picked up a battered phone and dialed a number.

"Tommy? This is Charlie over at the Globe. Listen, you know if Wallace has a new girl? Sort of a rookie type? A little weird—does fantasy acts . . ."

The four flights of stairs were narrow and foul-smelling, strewn with empty malt liquor bottles and cigarette butts. In the fourth floor hallway, two tired-looking women in their underwear shared a cigarette and a fifth of something pink. When Kathryn reached Room 44 she jabbed the key into the lock, felt the particleboard door shudder as she twisted the key. After a moment it sprang open, and they went inside.

The room looked no better or worse than its neighbors: dingy gray walls with a filigree of silverfish and crushed cockroaches, lumpy double bed, an ashtray that had not been emptied. Water trickled disconsolately from the bathroom tap, and the toilet ran. Cole walked over to the bed and sat down, exhausted. He closed his eyes and started to lean back onto the threadbare pillow, but Kathryn immediately began pacing back and forth, stopping every now and then to regard him with a sort of breathless wonder, as though still amazed to see him there.

"Okay, James—the last time I saw you, you were standing there looking at the moon, you were eating leaves—then what?"

Cole blinked, rubbed the dark stubble on his chin. "I thought—I thought I was in prison again."

Kathryn halted, regarding him through slitted eyes. "Just like that? You were in prison?"

Cole's brow furrowed. "No, not really." He looked

as though he were in pain. "It's—it's in my mind. Like you said."

Kathryn shook her head furiously and began pacing again. "No! *You disappeared!* One minute you were there, the next minute you were gone. Did you run through the woods?"

"I don't know. I—I don't remember."

Kathryn walked to the far wall and stared out a grimy window to the alley below. "The boy in the well." She turned, her pale eyes practically incandescent. "How did you know that was just a hoax?"

Cole frowned. "It was? I didn't—*know.*"

"James, you said he was hiding in the barn." Kathryn's voice rose in exasperation.

Cole bit his lip, frowned and stared intently at the ceiling. "I think I saw a TV show like that when I was a kid. Where a boy—"

"*It wasn't a TV show! It was real!*"

Cole sat up, surprised. With her ruined clothes and tangled hair and rabid expression, Kathryn Railly looked positively demented. He stared at her for a minute.

"Well, maybe that kid saw the same TV show and copied it," he said at last, slowly and with great care. He moved to the edge of the bed, his voice rising eagerly. "Because listen—you were right. It's all in my head. I'm mentally ill; I imagine all that stuff. I know they're not real. I can trick them, make them do what I want—" He snapped his fingers, then waved dismissively. "I just worked on them in my head and I got back here. I can get better. I can stay here."

He looked up at her with wide anxious eyes,

willing himself to be calm, to be well. Kathryn gazed back at him, suddenly stood and got her purse. She pulled out a manila envelope, and handed a large photo to Cole.

"What does this mean to you?"

It was the uncropped photo of the Latino boy in WWI, with Cole a fuzzy shadow at the edge of the frame. Cole stared at it bleakly. His expression changed from hope to confusion to genuine fear.

"I—I had a dream about—about something like that," he said at last, his voice breaking.

Kathryn took the photo back, nodding grimly. "You had a bullet from World War One in your leg, James. How did it get there?"

Cole began shaking his head, slowly at first, then faster and faster. "You said I had delusions—that I created a world—you said that you could explain everything."

Kathryn looked at him, white-faced. "Well, I can't. I mean, I'm trying to. I can't believe that everything we do or say has already happened, that we can't change what's going to happen—that I'm one of the five billion people who are going to die . . . soon."

Cole stood, moved closer to her. His eyes were bright with tears as he opened his arms, embracing the scuffed floor, the stained bedclothes, the leaden square of window with its slab of dull sky, Kathryn herself.

"I want to be here," he whispered. "In this time. With you. I want to become—to become a whole person. I want this to be the present. I want the future to be unknown."

He lifted his face. She saw in it more desperation than she had ever seen before; desperation and an almost frantic need to hope, to believe in something—to believe in her. She felt her heart clench inside her, fear like a poison spurting through her entire body. Unthinkingly she bunched her hands into fists and looked away from him, anything to not see his face pleading with her, begging her to save him.

Her eyes fell on the telephone.

"James," she said. Like a sleepwalker she pointed at the nightstand. "Do you remember—six years ago? You had a phone number? You tried to call and—"

Cole nodded slowly. "A lady answered."

"It was a wrong number in 1990," Kathryn said. She stared at the cheap plastic phone, as though willing it to ring. "But it should be the *right* number now. Do you—do you remember it? The number?"

Bam! A splintering crash as the door flew open. A looming figure half fell, half lunged into the room—a tall man with long hair and cracked leathers, his wiry arms and hands covered with jailhouse tattoos. He stood in the middle of the room, breathing heavily as he looked Kathryn up and down with cold ice-pale eyes.

"This is *my* territory, bitch!" he sneered, moving menacingly toward her.

Confused, Cole turned to Kathryn. "Is this real? Or is this one of my delusions?"

Shaking her head, Kathryn backed away. "This is definitely real." She looked at Wallace. "Excuse me, I think we have a little misunderstanding here—"

The biker smashed her in the face. With a moan Kathryn flew back against the wall, sliding to the floor as the biker spun around to face Cole.

"What're you—some kind of tough guy?" Grinning, the biker raised his hand. In it glinted a knife. "You wanna be a hero? You gonna try and mess with me? Come on . . . "

Cole hesitated, then raised his hands placatingly. He backed around Wallace and moved to where Railly leaned against the wall. She stared at him in dazed disbelief, gingerly touching an eye already as bruised and swollen as spoiled fruit.

"Now that's a smart boy." The biker nodded, tracing a circle in the air with his knife. His grin faded as he looked at Railly. "But *you*, honey—you think you can go round *me* and peddle your fancy ass in this part of town, you bet your life we got what you call a major goddamn understanding."

He started for her, knife extended. Kathryn cried out and reached for Cole. He pushed her hand away and snatched up her purse, swinging it so that it smashed into the biker's face. As the man staggered backward Cole grabbed his arm and pulled it straight up, then back. There was a straining sound, as if heavy cloth was being pulled apart, then a sharp crack. The man screamed, staring in horror at a jutting rim of bone protruding from his elbow. With a hollow clatter his knife fell to the floor.

"James," whispered Kathryn, her eyes wide.

Cole said nothing. Instead he lunged for the biker and pinned him to the floor, straddling his chest as he snatched up the knife and pressed it against the biker's neck.

Kathryn's stunned expression turned to horror. "James—*don't!*"

Cole hesitated.

"You—heard—her," the biker gasped, his eyes bulging. "Don't do it, man."

Shakily, Kathryn got to her feet. She ran a trembling hand across her face and looked around, focusing at last on a particleboard alcove with a warped door. She looked at Cole.

"Put him in the closet," she said. "But get his money first."

Cole stared at her in amazement. "You want me to *rob* him?"

Kathryn swallowed, then nodded. "I—I—we need cash, James."

She turned sharply as a shadow fell across the wall. For an instant the doorway framed a white slack face, its mouth a perfect O. Then the face disappeared, and shouts echoed from the hallway.

"*They're killing him! Call the cops!*"

Cole moved slightly where he straddled the biker, adjusted the knife so that it edged closer to the man's jugular. The man's eyes rolled wildly. Then, very carefully, so as not to disrupt the careful balance between knife and neck, his good arm twitched. Slowly he reached into his pocket and withdrew a thick wad of bills. Kathryn grabbed them and crossed quickly to the bed.

"You two are crazy," the biker said in a hoarse voice. His face contorted with pain. "I got friends—

you put me in a closet, they're gonna be really pissed."

In one fluid motion Cole stood, holding the knife threateningly in one hand as with the other he yanked the biker to his feet. The biker cried out, clutching at his limp arm. Kathryn rushed to the window and looked down. A rusted fire escape led down into an alley choked with old newspapers and beer cans.

"James—" she began. She glanced back in time to see Cole disappearing into the bathroom with Wallace. There was a small *click* as the door locked behind them.

"James!" she cried. Desperately she rattled the knob, put all her weight against the door. "Please—"

She could hear the biker's ugly voice, still refusing to plead with Cole. "I have friends, man—if you cut me—"

"James! Don't hurt him! *Please!*"

"I mean it, man, they'll— *Jesus Christ!* What the fuck are you *doing?*"

Tears running down her face, Kathryn pounded on the door. Suddenly it opened. She fell backward, catching herself against the wall as Cole stepped out. In his hand he gripped the knife. Blood dripped from it in slow strands, stained his hand all the way to the wrist. Kathryn covered her mouth.

"Oh, my God, James. Did you kill him?"

He shook his head. "Just—just in case," he said thickly. Blood oozed from his mouth as he spoke. "In case I'm *not* crazy . . ."

He held up two bloody prongs half as long as his

thumb. It was a moment before Kathryn realized she was staring at two of his molars.

"That's how they find us," he explained. Blood spotted the floor beneath him. "By our teeth."

He lifted his face and stared at her. And in spite of the blood and grime, his bloodshot eyes, the knife, and all the other madness, she saw him as if for the first time. Not a psychotic ex-con who had pursued her for six years, but another man entirely, a man who could weep at the rising moon and not seem pathetic, someone who still believed the old songs he heard on the radio, someone whose depth of feeling was not bound by time or space or even the subtle convolutions of the mind itself . . .

Someone who loved her.

For a long moment they stood there. And somehow Kathryn knew that this was it, the closest she would ever come to something she had long ago given up any hope of having: a thirty-five-dollar-an-hour room in a skid row flophouse, a pimp moaning in pain in the next room, and a bloodstained man gazing at her as though she were the Pieta. And somehow, somehow it was enough.

Abruptly the room shook. From the corridor came the thunder of booted feet thudding up the stairs.

"POLICE! THROW YOUR WEAPONS OUT AND COME OUTTA THERE!"

Silently Cole reached for her. She took his hand and followed him to the window, waited as he shoved it opened and slid outside, pulling her gently after him onto the fire escape.

"Hey! That the police? I'm an innocent victim in

here!" the biker shrieked from the bathroom. A uniformed cop charged into the room in a crouch, pistol extended in both hands. He panned the gun around an empty room. "Get me the fuck outta here! I was attacked by a coked-up whore and a crazy dentist!"

More policemen rushed in, kicking aside furniture as they raced for the open window and stared down into an alley where blood glowed like petals on the drifting piles of newsprint.

Holiday shoppers hurried toward the curb as a city bus pulled up, angling for the door with armfuls of bright shopping bags. The doors *whooshed* open, disgorging a late-afternoon crush onto the avenue. Overhead streamers of gold and green arced from one streetlight to the next, gleaming in the faint sunlight. White lights glittered from bare tree limbs in the first shadows of twilight. Along the avenue, canopies flapped in the wind and holiday crowds surged past expensive storefronts: Wanamaker's, Bloomingdale's, Neiman Marcus. There was music, the heady brazen burst of a Salvation Army band vying with the genteel tinkle of handbells playing *The Dance of the Sugarplum Fairies.*

The bus pulled away, leaving a haze of bluish exhaust. As the shoppers dispersed, Kathryn Railly moved furtively to the relative shelter of the crowded sidewalk. Sunglasses hid her bruised eye. Behind her Cole moved more slowly, a bloody handkerchief pressed to his mouth. He gazed at the hundreds of people, the shining store windows and laughing children with the stunned expression of a man waking from a troubled dream.

"Keep your head down and try to blend in," Kathryn whispered. She grabbed his hand and pulled him close to her. "We'll stick with the crowd. There's got to be a phone around here— There!" she said excitedly, pointing to a corner booth. "In there."

She hurried him past a chorus of blue-uniformed Salvation Army volunteers circling a shining scarlet kettle. Cole stopped and stared at them, shaking his head slowly.

"God rest ye merry, gentlemen,
Let nothing you dismay . . ."

Kathryn tugged at Cole's hand, but he refused to budge. The cold breeze brought with it the smell of fir trees and wood smoke, mingling with the music to prod at him with some faint memory almost within reach. He lifted his head, the music washing over him like rain, and gazed upward. His mouth fell open and his eyes widened, trapped somewhere between wonder and terror.

It was the building from his dream: the ornate and crumbling structure he had reached after emerging from the sewer, the building where he had seen snow and heard the distant baying of wolves. As he stared he saw silhouetted against its rococo roof a regal figure, gold-maned, its head thrown back so that the sun set its corona of hair aflame.

"James! Listen—"

He started, turned to see Kathryn dropping her hand from his, "I'm going to try that phone number you had. Let's hope it's nothing–"

Disoriented, he watched her hurry off, her dark hair disappearing and then popping into view again as the flow of Christmas shoppers streamed past. Some of them were close enough now that he could see their faces, their smiles and cheerfully generic holiday greetings suddenly frozen as they took in the dazed man standing there like the survivor of a car wreck. Cole pressed the handkerchief more tightly to his mouth and backed away. Someone jostled him and he fell against a shop window. Turning he recoiled in terror: inches from his face a bear reared on its hind legs, jaws bared in a snarl.

"James! James—"

Kathryn's voice filtered to him through the music and laughter. He shook his head, saw that the bear was only part of an elaborate display involving toy train trestles laden with fake snow, a mountainside where Lilliputian skiers slalomed through glittering powder.

"It's okay, James! We're insane! We're crazy!"

Laughing, Kathryn ran up to him, grabbed his hand, and hugged him clumsily. A passerby gave them an odd look, then shrugged and hurried on. "It's a carpet cleaning company."

Cole let her lead him back into the crowded sidewalk. "A carpet cleaning company?"

"No superiors! No scientists!" Kathryn threw her head back joyously. "No people from the future. It's just a carpet cleaning company. They have voice mail—you leave a message telling them when you want your carpet cleaned."

Cole shook his head slowly. "You . . . you left them a message?"

Kathryn grinned impishly. Her cheeks glowed bright red; she looked like a schoolgirl on the first day of winter vacation.

"I couldn't resist!" she went on breathlessly. "I was *so* relieved. Wait'll they hear this nutty woman telling them—they better watch out for the Army of the Twelve Monkeys—I told them the Freedom for Animals Association—"

Cole gazed in horror at her rosy face. In a voice taut with dread he began reciting along with her.

"The Freedom for Animals Association on Second Avenue is the secret headquarters of the Army of the Twelve Monkeys. They're the ones who are going to do it. I can't do anything more. I have to go now. Have a Merry Christmas."

Kathryn broke off and stared at Cole in confused disbelief. She looked over her shoulder at the phone booth twenty yards away. "You—you couldn't have heard me."

Cole gazed at her numbly. "They got your message, Kathryn," he said. He no longer saw her, only a circle of scowling faces, the tail-end of an audio tape flapping off its reel. "They played it for me. It was a bad recording . . . distorted. I didn't recognize your voice."

Kathryn's expression grew terrified as she suddenly grasped his meaning. "My God," she whispered.

From the street behind them a horn blared.

Shaken, Kathryn turned to see a uniformed cop staring from the window of a police cruiser as it inched along in the bumper-to-bumper traffic. The policeman squinted at something, his brow furrowing, then reached for his radio.

"Come on." Kathryn grabbed Cole and began hurrying to where a red canopy heralded the entrance to Bloomingdale's. They ran inside, nearly tripping over a woman holding a glass tray heavy with perfume flagons.

"Hey—!"

Kathryn went on, heedless of the looks they were getting from well-dressed customers. Cole followed her, blood spotting his shirt as he dabbed at his mouth with the soaked handkerchief. Kathryn pulled up in front of a startled clerk in an oversized cashmere sweater and bow tie.

"Men's clothing?" she demanded.

The clerk stared at her, then frowned and pointed to an escalator. "Second floor. To the right. But—can I help you?"

"No!" Kathryn called over her shoulder. She dragged Cole toward the escalator. He stumbled, clutching at the rail as the steps moved upward through billows of gossamer angel's hair and tinsel garlands.

When they reached the top, Kathryn plowed on without hesitation, until they reached a display of haughty male mannequins in paisley flannel briefs.

"Here," she said. She began pacing through rows of shirts and sweaters and trousers, stopping momentarily at a sale table to toss several things in Cole's direction.

He caught them clumsily, still following her blindly. A few yards away, behind a register, a clerk with the offended mien of a recent Harvard grad watched them with growing suspicion.

At a display for resort wear Kathryn tore a Hawaiian shirt from its hanger, grabbed the other things from Cole, and strode to the counter.

". . . and this." She glanced at the clerk, started to venture a smile, but thought better of it. Instead she turned to Cole. "Anything else?"

But Cole wasn't there. He stood several yards away, staring with huge frightened eyes at an immense Christmas tree. It loomed above the aisles of clothes and eager shoppers, branches laden with blown-glass globes and translucent crystal birds, delicate chains of gold and green, and crimson stars. At its very top was an angel with the pure face and spun-gold hair of a Renaissance painting, her outstretched arms shadowed by a pair of silvery wings. Cole's mouth parted as he gazed into her face, watching in resigned dread as her porcelain features crumbled and fell like snow upon his upturned cheeks, while overhead pigeons flapped noisily into the gloom of a disintegrating building.

"James."

Cole turned, still not seeing Kathryn where she stood at the counter with clothes heaped before her. Apologetically, miming annoyance, she looked back up at the clerk.

"I guess that's it," she said with false cheeriness.

The clerk flashed her a chilly smile. "Shall I put that on your account, ma'am?"

"No." She thrust her hand into her purse. "I'll pay cash." The clerk gaped as she began peeling bills from a huge wad. "What floor are the wigs on, please?"

The clerk rang everything up and began folding it neatly into sheets of tissue.

"That won't be necessary," Kathryn said, shoving the clothes into the waiting shopping bag. She turned and fled across the floor to Cole.

"Merry Christmas," the clerk called after her with a grimace. As they stepped onto another escalator, he reached for the telephone.

Night. The waning moon cast golden streaks upon the bare brown lawn in front of a warehouse, momentarily ignited a torn magazine cover lifted by the wind. Shadows gathered in empty windows covered with steel mesh and cardboard. In the parking lot sat a dirty white van, painted with grotesquely large silverfish and cockroaches and what looked like gigantic crabs, their antennae waving.

BUGMOBILE
YOU PAY WE SPRAY

Inside the van, light flared as a flashlight played across a small circle of excited faces. Moonglow sifted through the window, gilded the smooth curve of Teddy's shaven scalp, the ankh tattooed on his cheek. In the near-darkness the ghostly faces of the other five activists hovered above their black-clad torsos.

"So then he goes into this incredible riff about how his shrink, like, replicated his brain while he was in the nuthouse. Turned it into a computer."

Teddy laughed, delighted at his own incredible tale, and leaned back on his haunches. A heavy leather belt circled his hips, weighted down with socket wrenches, hammers, and a heavy welding torch. The others were freighted with similar paraphernalia: pipe cutters, flares, rock-climbing gear.

"And Fale *believed* it?"

Teddy threw his hands up. "Oh, you know Fale! He's like, 'If you guys get nailed—and I'm sure you will—I never saw you before in my life!'"

Laughter all around, cut short by a sharp, rhythmic series of raps on the side door.

"Whoa, Nellie," one of the women whispered, and quickly slid the door open.

In the moonlight stood Jeffrey, grinning broadly. "Good morning, campers!" Behind him, three more activists staggered out of the darkness, lugging a huge, squirming black garbage bag.

"Awwwrighhht!"

"Far out, man. . . . "

Teddy leaned out, helped pick up the writhing bag and maneuvered it into the van. It lay quivering on the floor, like a gigantic pupa. Jeffrey and the other activists scrambled through the door, pushing their way to the front.

"Let's do it!"

The van shuddered to life, lumbered out of the parking lot and up onto a nearby entrance ramp to the freeway. The garbage bag continued to squirm and groan as Jeffrey crouched by the front seat, using a penlight to trace a route on a city map.

"Okay, that's stage one," he announced dramatically, pointedly ignoring the bag behind him. "In stage two, Monkey Four is over here—"

Teddy and several of the others watched the twitching bag with growing dismay. "What's the harm of opening it?" Teddy asked, once they were safely on the highway. "His eyes are taped, right?"

Jeffrey looked up, shrugged cheerfully. He thrust his map into the driver's lap and leaned back over the bag, grabbing it with both hands and ripping it open. Black plastic fell away to reveal the trussed figure of Dr. Leland Goines, his mouth and eyes covered with silvery duct tape.

Jeffrey grinned wickedly. "Want the full effect?"

Before anyone could reply, he ripped the tape from his father's mouth. Dr. Goines moaned, his blind head tossing back and forth, then cried out hoarsely.

"Jeffrey? I know it's you, Jeffrey. I recognize your voice."

Jeffrey put a finger to his lips and looked around, commanding the others to silence.

"Jeffrey?" Dr. Goines' tongue flicked out over his dry mouth. His body shook with a spasm of coughing. "Very well. I know all about your insane plan. That woman—your psychiatrist—she told me."

Jeffrey raised his eyebrows in surprise, fought to keep his dismay from showing as his father went on, his blinded face eerie in the dimness.

"I didn't believe her—it seemed too crazy even for you. But, just in case, I took steps to make sure you couldn't do it. I don't have the code anymore—I don't have access! I took myself out of the loop! *I don't have access to the virus.* So go ahead—torture me, kill me, do whatever you want. It won't do any good."

Above his now-still figure the other activists drew together, exchanging puzzled, even frightened, looks. Jeffrey turned to them, throwing his hands up in mock horror.

"The loop?" he cried. "The loopy scientist takes himself out of *the loop?"* He laughed, loudly and incredulously, as Teddy and the others moved to the other side of the van.

Dr. Goines' head spun, following the sound of Jeffrey's voice. "I would never let myself believe it," he said, his voice as thin and shrill as an old woman's. "I mean, I could never truly believe it—my own son—but I know it now. . . . "

He spat the final words, so that even Jeffrey's face grew pinched to hear him.

"Jeffrey . . . *you are completely insane."*

In the darkness ahead of them a sign loomed: PHILADELPHIA ZOO, NEXT EXIT.

"Shut up," Jeffrey said, kicking at his father's bound form. "Shut up, shut up, shut up. . . ."

The others cowered in the corner as Jeffrey ranted on and on, his voice rising dangerously as the van lurched onto the turnoff for the zoo.

Eerie music filled the theater where scarcely a dozen people sat, refugees from the cold or the holidays or even worse. On screen, vast redwoods soared sky-ward, dwarfing two tiny figures strolling through the forest.

"I know that guy," James Cole said, his voice momentarily drowning Stewart's. He craned his neck as Kathryn tugged at the collar of his new shirt. "And her, too."

"Shhhh!" whispered someone behind them

"Here's a cross section of one of the old trees that's been cut down." Stewart sidled up in front of the huge slab of wood. Beside him Kim Novak gazed at the cards indicating the tree's age at various points during its eons-long life.

BIRTH OF CHRIST
DISCOVERY OF AMERICA
MAGNA CARTA SIGNED
1066—BATTLE OF HASTINGS
1930—TREE CUT DOWN

Kim Novak pointed, her voice deeply melancholy. *"Somewhere in here I was born. And here—I die. There's only a moment for you. You don't notice."*

"Here, James—let me help you."

Kathryn pulled something from her purse and began rubbing it on Cole's upper lip. He fidgeted like a child, trying to see the screen. "I think I've seen this movie before. When I was a kid. It was on TV."

Kathryn frowned, still fussing with his lip. "Sssh—don't talk. Hold still."

"I *have* seen it, but I don't remember this part. Funny, it's like what's happening to us, like the past."

For a moment he sat still, staring raptly at the screen. "The movie never changes—it can't change—but every time you see it, it seems to be different because *you're* different. You notice different things."

Kathryn stopped, let her hands fall into her lap. She looked at his boyish face, entranced by the film, and slowly lifted one hand and let it rest upon his cheek.

"If we *can't* change anything," she whispered, "because it's already happened, then we ought to at least smell the flowers."

"Flowers?" Cole turned and looked at her, surprised. "*What* flowers?"

"SHHHH!"

Kathryn glanced apologetically behind them, then reached for the shopping bag at her feet. "It's just an expression. Here—"

She pulled something from the bag and placed it on Cole's head, frowning as she adjusted it. Cole looked at her, no longer childlike, merely exhausted.

"Why are we doing this?"

Kathryn took his hands in hers and spoke fiercely. "So we can stick our heads out the window and feel the wind and listen to the music. So we can appreciate what we have while we have it." Her voice broke and she turned away. "Forgive me. Psychiatrists don't cry."

The wash of light from the movie screen made her eyes glow, bright with tears. Cole watched her, discomfited; finally he shook his head.

"But maybe I'm wrong. Maybe *you're* wrong. Maybe we're *both* crazy."

Kathryn stared resolutely at the seat in front of them, hands clutching at her knees. "In a few weeks, it will have started or it won't. If there are still football games and traffic jams, armed robberies and boring TV shows—we'll be so happy, we'll be *glad* to turn ourselves in to the police."

"SHHHH!"

Cole slumped down in his seat, whispering, "But where can we hide for a few weeks?"

On the screen above them, Jimmy Stewart and Kim Novak paused. The sounds of waves echoed through the theater, and wind tossed Novak's pale hair. Kathryn lifted her face to Cole's.

"You said you'd never seen the ocean."

He took her in his arms, then, burying his face in her hair and saying her name, over and over again, heedless of the hushed protests behind them.

> *"Oh, Papa's gonna take us to the zoo tomorrow*
> *Zoo tomorrow, zoo tomorrow*
> *Papa's gonna take us to the zoo tomorrow*
> *And we can stay all day . . ."*

Through the moonlit trees wafted Jeffrey Goines' voice, followed by a chorus of angry whispers.

"Christ, Jeffrey, don't blow it now!"

"Shut up!"

"*You* shut up!"

The shadowy figures halted beneath a barren oak tree, its branches scraping at the sky. Their voices began to rise angrily again, when from the darkness came a rustling sound, the bellow of some furious creature and then a man's plaintive voice.

"Where are you? What are you doing to me? Jeffrey, please—"

The voice was cut off by an ominous guttural snarl. In the tangled shadows of the oak, the little cluster of activists drew quickly together.

"Uh, Jeffrey . . ." came an urgent whisper. "You think maybe—"

Jeffrey's voice rang out, followed by another snarl, closer this time. "I think we better get the hell outta Dodge," he cried, and sprinted toward the zoo entrance as an immense shape emerged from the shrubs behind him. The others turned and followed him, racing to the van.

He is standing on the same beach where Jimmy Stewart had stood moments before. In the near distance, waves crash upon the shore. A bird keens overhead. He nudges at the sand with his bare feet, frowning slightly—what does sand feel like?—then looks up. The bird's cry grows louder, more menacing. He sees that the sky clouded, the sun blotted out by a sudden pandemonium of wings, rustling, thrashing wings and the clatter of metal on metal, cages opening as the sound of birds builds to a screeching crescendo. With a cry Cole lurched forward, bumping his head against the seat in front of him. Moaning, he looked up.

Birds. Everywhere, birds, and a blond woman screaming, crouched in a small room as screeching beaks and wings battered at her upraised arms.

"Kathryn?"

Cole stumbled to his feet, looking around in a panic. The theater was empty.

"Kathryn!"

He fell into the aisle and ran, limping, back toward the lobby. Flickering lights cast a hazy glow on worn flocked wallpaper, the prone figure of the theater's elderly usher snoring in his velvet chair, peeling posters boasting CLASSICS 24 HOURS A DAY and HITCH-COCK FESTIVAL!!! There were no other moviegoers; only a blond woman talking on the lobby's pay phone. Cole staggered into the middle of the room, looking around wildly. With a muffled *clink* the blonde hung up the phone, turned, and called to him.

"We're booked on a nine-thirty flight to Key West."

Cole stared at her in shock. Kathryn, but not Kathryn; her dark hair was hidden beneath a blond wig, eyes heavily mascaraed and mouth frosted with bright red lipstick. She wore brassy gold costume jewelry around her neck and huge hoop earrings, a tight flowered skirt and blouse, and red high-heeled shoes. Cole shook his head and took a step backward, still looking around as though the *real* Kathryn might suddenly turn up. That was when he saw his own reflection in one of the lobby's smoked mirrors: a muscular man in a gaudy Hawaiian shirt, with a mustache and hair as blond as the woman's. He touched his face, confused, his fingers gingerly feeling the stiff hairs on his upper lip. Finally he turned back to Kathryn, shamefaced.

"I didn't recognize you."

She smiled and walked until she stood beside him. "Well, you look pretty different, too."

"In my dream—" He touched her cheek, gently, moved his hand to caress her temple "—it's always been you."

She studied him, her pale eyes serious. "I remember you like this," she said at last. "I felt I've known you before. I feel I've always known you."

They stood gazing at each other, the rippling voices from the movie rising and falling around them like waves. Then, Kathryn backed up, pulling Cole after her as she maneuvered past the sleeping usher, past the abandoned refreshment stand and rows of stanchions, until they reached an unmarked door that stood slightly ajar. Still silent, she pulled the door open and they were inside. In the half-darkness Cole saw plastic trash barrels, brooms, walls covered with old movie posters.

"James . . ."

She tugged at the shirt she had so carefully dressed him in, pulling it open so that she could run her hands across his chest. He moaned and crushed her to him, tilted her head back until he found her mouth and he kissed her, the two of them collapsing onto the floor amidst the tangled detritus of a thousand dark afternoons and sunless mornings. She moved beneath him and Cole tore her clothes away, the too-bright blouse and jewelry and the golden wig, his hands moving frantically over her body as though to find the other woman, the one he even now feared he had lost, the one he had fought his whole life to find, over and over again.

Afterward they slept, dozing fitfully among the stacks of ancient theater seats. It was Kathryn who woke first, peering worriedly out the closet door and seeing the usher still sound asleep.

"James!" she whispered. "We have to go."

He stirred, groaning softly, but sat up smiling when he saw her.

"I was dreaming," he said. "But a different dream, this time. Do you think that means anything?"

She smoothed the front of her skirt, then reached to give Cole's wig a tug, eyeing him critically. "I think we better get out of here before Sleeping Beauty out there wakes up."

They crept from the storage closet and made their way back into the theater. The opening credits of *Vertigo* were rolling again. Hurrying down the aisle they passed another couple, a boy and a girl sleeping soundly in each other's arms. Cole stared at them wistfully, then turned to Kathryn and smiled.

"Key West, huh? So I'll finally see the ocean . . ."

Outside, the first wan light of a winter morning was seeping down the sides of buildings. A delivery truck rolled past, a man in the back hurling newspapers across the sidewalk to land in front of locked doors. From a cafe down the street came the smells of coffee and baked goods. Cole gazed longingly in that direction, but Kathryn was already striding into the street and flagging down a cab.

"James—over here—"

Behind the wheel a fiftyish woman with white hair and a plaid jacket greeted him. "Don't keep the lady waiting, hon," she drawled in a thick Southern twang. "What time's your flight, friends?"

Cole shrugged and looked at Kathryn, resplendently blond once more in sunglasses and gleaming lipstick.

"Nine-thirty," she said, patting Cole's knee and grinning.

The cab shot out into the street. "Might be tight," the driver announced.

Kathryn looked startled. "Tight?" She glanced at her wrist. "My watch says seven thirty."

The cabbie nodded. "On your normal mornin', okay, plenty a time, but today, you gotta take inta account your Army-of-the Twelve-Monkeys factor."

Kathryn froze. "*What?* What did you say?"

The cabbie glanced back at them. "Twelve Monkeys, honey. Guess you folks didn't turn on your radio this morning." She lit a cigarette, then went on.

"Buncha weirdos let all the animals outta the zoo last night. Then they locked up this big-shot scientists in one of the cages. Scientist's own kid was one 'a the ones that did it!" she cackled. Cole and Kathryn stared at her, stunned. "Now they got animals all over the place! Buncha zebras down the Schuylkill 'bout an hour ago and some kinda thing called an 'ee-moo' got traffic blocked for miles over on Route 676."

Kathryn turned wildly to Cole. "That's all they were up to! Freeing animals!"

Cole began to nod, slowly. "On the walls—they meant the animals when they said, 'We did it.'"

The cabbie grinned and switched on the radio.

With a cry Cole pointed out the window. Kathryn whirled to see a neighboring freeway, traffic at a dead standstill, police and traffic helicopters hovering overhead. Down the median strip, their heads moving up and down like those of carousel animals, loped three giraffes.

"—*and now we have one of the many animal rights activists who are critical of the so-called Twelve Monkeys*—"

A second, angrier voice blared from the speaker. "*Can these fools seriously believe that releasing an animal into an urban environment is being compassionate to the animal? It's mindlessly cruel, almost as indefensible as holding the animal in captivity in the first place.*"

Outside, skyscrapers glittered in the morning sun. As Kathryn and Cole watched, a flock of flamingos rose from a thicket and arrowed across the sky. Cole's hand covered hers as she gazed at the sun-colored birds and whispered, "Maybe it's going to be okay."

They rode in silence the rest of the way. When they reached the airport the cabbie waved as Cole and Kathryn slid from the car.

"Watch out for them monkeys," she drawled.

Kathryn smiled. "Oh, we will."

The two of them hurried inside, past waiting skycaps and businessmen. The terminal was crowded, enough so that they walked unnoticed past a ticket counter where a paunchy man in plainclothes was handing flyers to the counter supervisor.

"Thanks, Detective Dalva," the supervisor said, and studied the photocopied images.

Dalva turned to go. "Tell your people if they spot either one of them, not to try and apprehend them.

They should notify us through airport security." He walked off briskly, disappearing into the crowd.

Not far off, Kathryn paused to scrutinize an information kiosk, teetering somewhat uncomfortably on her high heels. Beside her Cole stared at the immense terminal stretching all around them, the huge observation windows and knots of people hurrying toward their gates. From overhead a woman's voice rang out over the PA system.

"Flight 531 for Chicago is now ready for boarding at Gate Seventeen . . ."

Cole shook his head, shocked. "I know this place! This is my dream!"

Kathryn continued to gaze at the kiosk, frowning. "Airports all look the same," she said tersely. "Maybe it's—"

She turned and gasped. "James! Your mustache—it's slipping."

"It's not just my dream," Cole went on. He didn't look at her. "I was actually here! I remember now. My parents brought me to meet my uncle. About a week or two before . . . before . . . before everyone started dying," he ended in a whisper.

Kathryn stepped back from the kiosk, glancing around nervously. At the other end of the lobby she spied two uniformed policemen strolling side by side, scanning the faces of passing travelers.

"They may be looking for us, James," she said quickly. She opened her purse, pulled out a small tube of spirit gum, and handed it to him. "Here—use this to fix your mustache. You can do it in the men's room."

But Cole was still staring at the observation windows. "I was here as a kid," he said, his voice detached, almost dreamy. "I think you were here, too. But you you looked just like you look now."

Kathryn shook his arm desperately. "James, if we're identified, they're going to send us someplace—but *not* to Key West!"

All of a sudden he snapped out of it. "Right! You're right—I have to fix it." He stroked his mustache and nodded.

"I'll get the tickets and meet you—" Kathryn glanced at the top of an escalator, then at a small arcade at its bottom "—in the gift shop."

Cole waited until she started for the escalator, watching her long-legged stride and tight skirt attract admiring leers from a group of boys in matching college sweats. Then he headed for the men's room.

He was almost there when he saw the pay phones, a long line of glass-and-steel cubicles against the wall. Business travelers were hunched in all the alcoves but one. Cole hesitated, took another step, and stopped. He bit his lip, felt his mustache move another fraction of an inch. Quickly he pushed it back into place. He nodded to himself, jamming his hand into his pocket, and hurried for the empty booth. He slid several coins awkwardly into the slot, waited, then dialed, listening as an answering machine clicked on. When the message ended he began to talk into the phone curtly in a very low voice, his expression extraordinarily intense.

"This is Cole, James. Listen, I don't know whether you're there or not. Maybe you just clean carpets. If you do, you're lucky—you're gonna live a long, happy life. *But*—if you other guys exist and you're picking this up—forget about the Army of the Twelve Monkeys. They didn't do it. It was a mistake! Someone else did it. The Army of the Twelve Monkeys is just a bunch of dumb kids playing revolutionaries."

Glancing around nervously, he caught the businessman at the next phone quickly averting his eyes. Cole touched his loose mustache again, talking into the phone in an urgent whisper.

"I've done my job. I did what you wanted. Good luck. I'm not coming back."

He hung up and looked around again, saw several people staring at him curiously. Ducking his head, he headed quickly for the men's room.

Inside, Cole stood with his head bowed in front of a sink. He washed his hands methodically as he waited for another traveler to leave. The PA system droned as the other man finished up, gave Cole a quizzical look, and left.

As soon as he was gone, Cole glanced around. Seeing no one else he withdrew the tube of spirit gum from his pocket, squirted some of the goop under the loose edge of his mustache, and pressed it firmly against his face. He leaned up against the mirror, squinting to make sure it would remain in place this time.

"Got yourself a prob, Bob?" a familiar voice rasped.

With a choked gasp Cole whirled, looking around frantically for the source of the voice. Nothing—

until at the bottom of one stall he spotted a pair of wing tip shoes peeking from beneath dropped trousers.

"Leave me alone!" cried Cole. "I made a report. I didn't have to do that."

The voice gave a throaty, ominous chuckle. "Point of fact, Bob—you don't belong here. It's not permitted to let you stay."

Cole shouted his reply above the gurgling thunder of a flushing toilet. "This is the present! This is not the past. This is not the future. This is *right now!*"

The door of the occupied stall swung open. Out stepped a plump businessman, his eyes fixed warily on Cole as he gave him a wide berth on his way to the sink.

"I'm staying here!" Cole yelled. "You got that? *You can't stop me!*"

Changing his mind, the man skirted the sink and made straight for the door. "Anything you say, chief," he said in a reedy, high-pitched voice. "It's none of my business."

Cole looked after him, dismayed, then turned and peered under the other stalls, looking for signs of life. Had he imagined the voice? Was this the beginning of another one of his terrible dreams? He fled the men's room, intent only on finding Kathryn and not leaving her side again.

Back in the main terminal it was even more crowded than it had been just a few minutes earlier. The echoing announcements of flights continued almost without pause. Cole looked around, shaken. Keeping his head down he started for the escalator, hoping to intercept Kathryn there. Suddenly someone grabbed his shoulder from behind.

"You gotta be crazy, man!"

He tried to shake loose, turned and saw a young Puerto Rican man in a Raiders jacket, sideways baseball cap, and mirrored sunglasses.

"Jo—Jose?" Cole stammered.

Jose shook his head seriously as people brushed past them. "Pulling out the teeth, man—that was nuts! Here, take this—"

He edged closer to Cole, trying to slide a 9mm pistol into his hand. Cole stared at him in disbelief and pulled away.

"*What?* What for? Are you crazy?" He batted at Jose's hand, glancing around with wild eyes. Frustrated, Jose shoved the gun back under his jacket, then grabbed Cole's arm tightly.

"Me? Are you kiddin'? *You're* the one!" His eyes glittered as he gazed into Cole's face. "You were a hero, man. They gave you a pardon! And whadda you do? You come back and fuck with your teeth! Wow!" Jose's voice died into admiring astonishment.

"How did you find me?"

Jose edged closer to Cole, letting a cloud of Hare Krishnas float by. "The phone call, man," he said in a low voice. "The phone call. They did their reconstruction thing on it."

"The call I just made?" Cole asked incredulously. "Five minutes ago?"

Jose shrugged. "Hey, five minutes ago, thirty years ago! They just put it together."

He made his tone deeper, imitating Cole. "'This is

Cole, James. I don't know whether you're there or not. Maybe you just clean carpets.' Ha ha." He elbowed Cole, shaking his head ruefully. "Clean carpets? Where'd you get that? 'Forget about the Army of the Twelve Monkeys.' If they coulda got your message earlier . . ."

Jose's voice died. He looked at Cole, his face torn between anger and a certain wistfulness, and once again pressed the pistol into his hand. "Here—take it, man! You could *still* be a hero if you'd cooperate!"

Cole pushed him away and half walked, half ran to the escalator. He stepped on, hugging himself to the railing as the stairs slid downward, trying to ignore Jose.

"Come on, Cole, don't be an asshole," he begged. Cole stared stonily ahead of him, trying to will his heart to slow its pounding. For a long moment both were silent. Then:

"Look, I got orders, man!" Jose blurted. "You know what I'm s'posed to do if you don't go along? I'm s'posed to shoot the lady! You got that? They said, 'If Cole don't obey this time, Garcia, you gotta shoot his girlfriend!'"

Stunned, Cole spun around to face his friend.

"I got no choice, man," pleaded Jose. "These are my orders. Just take it, okay?"

Cole shook his head, mouth open to speak, but no words came. He turned away from Jose, staring numbly at the Up escalator beside them—and saw there the microbiologist, his face hidden by square black glasses, his spare frame clad in a sober business suit. As Cole watched, he lifted his glasses and gazed implacably at him with narrowed eyes the color of dirty ice as the escalator carried him away. Very slowly, Cole turned back to Jose on the step behind him.

"This part isn't about the virus, is it?" His face showed nothing as Jose slid the gun into his hand.

"Hey, man—"

"It's about obeying, about doing what you're told." The escalator reached the bottom and Cole stumbled off.

"They gave you a pardon, man," Jose called after him imploringly. "Whaddya want?"

Cole said nothing. He shoved the pistol into his trouser pocket and started walking blindly toward the gift shop, Jose running to keep up.

At the ticket counter, Kathryn stood in line, her eyes unreadable behind her sunglasses, her mouth twisted into a tight rictus of a smile. In front of her, a cluster of tourists traveling together finally finished their business and moved away. Kathryn stepped up, trying to look like someone beginning the vacation of a lifetime.

"Judy Simmons," she said brightly. "I have reservations for Key West."

The ticket agent flashed her an automatic smile and punched numbers into a computer. "Here you are," she announced as the printer began spitting out tickets. "And how will you be paying for this?"

Kathryn's stomach churned, her mouth felt sore from smiling. "Like this!" she said cheerfully, pulling a stack of bills from her wallet.

The agent laughed. "Ooooh—we don't see a lot of *this*. Cash, I mean."

Kathryn made a funny little face. "It's a long story."

The agent counted out the bills, made a final pass at the keyboard, and handed over the tickets. "They'll begin boarding in about twenty minutes," she said, smiling. "Have a nice flight, Ms. Simmons."

Kathryn turned away, too quickly, hoping that the agent wouldn't notice her shaking hands, and immediately dropped the tickets. The woman in line behind her edged past as she frantically tried to gather everything. Breathless, Kathryn got back to her feet, leaning precariously on her high heels and praying that her wig hadn't slipped. She glanced back at the line to see if anyone had noticed, but everyone was arranged much as before, their faces ranging from impatience to indifference as they nudged their luggage across the floor. Hurriedly she stepped away and nearly tripped on something; when she glanced down, she saw her heel entangled in the strap of a bulky Chicago Bulls sports bag.

"Oh! I'm so sorry, excuse me—" she gasped, lifting her foot and stepping away. The bag remained where it was, resting against a leg clad in an unbelievably tacky pair of baggy plaid pants. Its owner didn't even glance at her.

"*Excuse* me." Another ticket agent squeezed by as Kathryn tried to get past the line, making sure she didn't trip over the bag again.

But the bag was gone. Kathryn cast a quick nervous look at the counter, worried that the man might have taken some notice of her. But she saw only those incredible pants, and thinning red hair pulled into a ponytail that formed a limp question mark against the back of the man's vivid shirt. His Chicago Bulls bag was shoved against the counter in front of him.

"Wooo-eee!" The ticket agent produced a pile of tickets several inches thick and flipped through them in awe. "San Francisco, New Orleans, Rio de Janeiro, Kinshasa, Karachi, Bangkok, Peking! That's some trip you're taking, sir—all in one week!"

The man shrugged. "Business."

The agent slid the stack across the counter. "Have a good one, sir." As the man turned, Kathryn looked away again, then started for the gift shop, her heels beating a rapid tattoo on the floor.

The shop was crowded. Kathryn scanned the faces: no Cole. She looked at her watch, closed her eyes, and took a deep breath.

Nothing is going to happen. Nothing is going to go wrong. You're going to meet him and get on that plane and by tonight you'll be toasting the sunset on the beach.

She opened her eyes, reconfigured her face with a smile, and stepped over to the travel section. She picked up a book on Key West. Then she sidled over to the magazines.

"Flight 272 to Houston now boarding at Gate . . ."

Once more she checked anxiously for the time.

Where is he?

She bit her lip, tasting the unfamiliar chalky taint of lipstick, then walked over to the cash register. She looked down, craning her neck to read the stacks of newspapers piled there, and so she did not see the ponytailed man in line in front of her, holding the latest *Sports Illustrated*. Instead she edged closer to the newspapers, frowning as she read the screaming headlines:

ANIMALS SET FREE!
PROMINENT SCIENTIST FOUND
LOCKED IN GORILLA CAGE

Beneath the subhead were two photos. One showed Dr. Leland Goines, his face ashen and strained, being helped from a cage by several policemen. The other photo showed a triumphant Jeffrey Goines, grinning maniacally as he raised his two cuffed hands—one making the "V" for victory, the other flipping the photographer the bird.

"Excuse me—"

She started as a man elbowed her, his bag knocking into her leg. Looking up she frowned.

It was the ponytailed man with the Chicago Bulls bag and the awful pants, the same man she had seen a few minutes earlier at the ticket counter. But now for the first time she could see his face, pasty and rather furtive, wisps of pale red hair sticking across his forehead.

I've seen him before, where have I seen him . . . ?

"Next!" urged the man behind the register. Kathryn turned back to the counter as the clerk rang up her magazines.

"That'll be six ninety-eight."

She paid him. Then, still bothered, she glanced back in time to see the ponytailed man's face in silhouette as he paused to scan a newspaper.

She gasped as it came back to her: the crowded reception room at Breitrose Hall, a lanky red-haired man bullying his way to the table, his scrawled ID card bearing the name DR. PETERS as he announced self-importantly:

"Isn't it obvious that 'Chicken Little' represents the sane vision, and that Homo sapiens' motto, 'Let's go shopping!' is the cry of the true lunatic?"

For a full minute she stood there, too shocked to move or do anything but watch the ponytailed man saunter off.

"Yo, miss—you mind moving a little?"

Nodding weakly, Kathryn stepped aside as a delivery man shoved a bundle of newspapers onto the stack beside her. As he walked away she looked down and read:

TERRORISTS CREATE CHAOS

The photos beneath the banner showed a rhino standing proudly in the middle of gridlocked traffic. Two other photos flanked it. One showed Dr. Goines in the gorilla cage. The other was a file photo of him in his lab, standing beside another man, his white lab coat covering most of a dark T-shirt, his pale hair pulled into a ponytail. As Kathryn stared, uncomprehending at first, the face of Goines' assistant became clear to her.

He was the man at her lecture. The man in line at the ticket counter.

The man with the ponytail and the Chicago Bulls bag.

"Oh, my God!" she cried aloud, looking around desperately for him.

But Dr. Peters was gone.

". . . Flight 784 for San Francisco is now ready for boarding at Gate Thirty-eight."

In the main terminal, Cole hurried toward the gift shop, his mouth tight as Jose tried to keep up with him.

"Who am I supposed to shoot?" he demanded, but just then Kathryn came running up, clutching her purse and a pile of magazines.

"James! Dr. Goines' assistant!" she said breathlessly. "He's an—an apocalypse nut! I think he's involved." She gestured wildly at a looming corridor where a line of metal detectors stood, surrounded by travelers and blue-uniformed security guards. "The next flight to San Francisco leaves from Gate Thirty-eight. If he's there, I'm *sure* he's part of it!"

Cole looked down into Kathryn's strained face, then to where Jose was stepping backward, melting into the crowd. He had one last glimpse of Jose's eyes as he pointed at Kathryn and nodded, slowly and with immeasurable gravity. Then he was gone. Abruptly, Cole was yanked away as Kathryn pulled him toward the security checkpoint.

"Maybe we can stop him," she said, her voice thin and unsteady. "Maybe we can actually do something. . . ."

Cole gazed at her, nodding, his eyes pricking with tears as he tried to pull it all into focus one last time:

the blond woman, her own pale eyes revealed momentarily as she pulled her sunglasses aside and stared frantically at the security gate; the airport bustling with its first surge of holiday travelers; the observation windows where a line of dark silhouettes stood watching the deceptively calm trajectory of jets across the blue sky.

"I love you, Kathryn," he whispered. "Remember that . . ."

She did not look at him, or even seem to have heard him, as she pulled him after her toward the gate.

They joined the line. Cole moved like a sleep-walker, the endless echoing drone of the gate announcements buzzing in counterpoint to the pulsing of his heart. Beside him Kathryn fidgeted, but he watched numbly as each traveler stepped up to the steely arch, setting luggage and pocketbooks and cameras, stuffed animals and skis and all the other detritus of an ordinary day onto the conveyor belt. As they neared the front of the line, he saw a small boy dart in front of his parents, flashing them a grin as he proudly marched through the magnetic arch-way. In his pocket, Cole's hand tightened against the butt of the pistol as he watched his six-year-old self walk out of sight, into a future he could never have imagined.

"*. . . Bags face down, please. Face down . . .*"

Beside Cole, Kathryn stood anxiously on tiptoe, trying and failing to get a view beyond the knot of travelers ahead of them.

"Oh, God, we don't have time for this," she said.

Where the crowd was thickest several yards away, an airport security guard and a paunchy police detective stood with their backs turned to the mob, carefully surveying passengers as they bent to retrieve their luggage.

". . . *Face down, please. Face down . . .*"

A man slung a bulging Chicago Bulls bag onto the belt and moved briskly through the arch. As the bag passed through the X-ray machine, the airline security officer staring at the monitor frowned.

"Excuse me, sir. Would you mind letting me have a look at the contents of your bag?"

On the other side of the arch Dr. Peters stopped, raising his eyebrows in mild surprise.

"Me? Oh, yes, of course. My samples. I have the appropriate papers."

He stepped aside, glancing placatingly at the suddenly stalled line behind him. The security guard motioned him to a table. Dr. Peters unpacked his bag, lining up six metal cylinders, along with a change of clothes and a Walkman.

"Biological samples," he explained with an apologetic smile. "I have the paperwork right here—"

He held up a sheaf of official-looking documents. Meanwhile, the security officer examined one of the tubes, turning it over and over in his hands and squinting, puzzled. Finally he said, "I'm going to have to ask you to open this, sir."

"Open it?" Dr. Peters blinked stupidly. "Oh! Well, of course—"

He took the metal cylinder and started to unscrew it. Behind them came the sound of raised voices. Dr.

Peters paid no attention, but the security officer turned away, scowling.

A woman had stepped from the line and was gesturing excitedly at another guard. A leggy blond woman, wearing flashy clothes and jewelry that even from that distance looked fake. The security officer glanced at where Detective Dalva and the airport detective stood watching the commotion with interest, then turned back to his inspection.

"Here! You see?" With a flourish Dr. Peters pulled a glass tube out of the metal cylinder and held it up to the light. "Biological! Check the papers—it's all proper. I have a permit."

The security officer stared at the sealed clear glass tube. "It's empty!"

Dr. Peters nodded slyly. "Well, yes, to be sure, it *looks* empty! But I assure you, it's not."

From the line came the echo of angry voices. Once again the security officer looked back.

"Please listen to me," pleaded Kathryn, still arguing with the other guard. "This is very urgent!"

The security officer shook his head patiently. "You'll have to get in line, ma'am."

"We're all in a hurry, lady!" yelled an aggrieved businessman. "What's so special about you?"

Shrugging, the security officer looked away. "Holidays. They make people crazy, you know?"

Dr. Peters smiled benignly, producing glass tubes from the remaining five cylinders as the security officer examined his paperwork.

"You see!" Dr. Peters waved a hand at the neat little line of crystal vials. "Also invisible to the naked eye!" Suddenly he grinned and swept up one of the glass tubes. Leaning toward the security officer, he opened it and waved it beneath the man's nose. "See!" He chuckled. "It doesn't even have an odor."

The security officer looked up from the sheaf of papers, glanced at the seemingly empty vial, and smiled.

"That's not necessary, sir." He returned the papers. "Here you go. Thanks for your cooperation. Have a good flight."

Hastily Dr. Peters snatched up all his tubes and vials, shoving them into his gym bag. He glanced back to where the same blond woman was raging at the now-irate security guard.

"Who you calling a moron, lady?"

Suddenly, from behind the woman a blond man stepped: muscular, wearing a garish Hawaiian shirt. "Get your hands off her!" he said in a cold voice.

The security guard backed away from Kathryn, stiffening and glancing over his shoulder for reinforcements. Beside the metal detector, Detective Dalva and the airport detective stood with arms crossed, watching the fracas intently. Suddenly, Detective Dalva frowned.

"James . . ." Kathryn whispered, her hand brushing his arm.

Instinctively Cole reached for his mustache, felt its feathery touch too low on his upper lip. For an instant his eyes linked with the detective's; then Cole looked away. On the other side of the metal arch Dr. Peters grabbed his bag and hurried off.

"Hold it! Just a moment—"

Dr. Peters froze, his face suddenly gone white. He turned, slowly, to see the security officer approaching, waving a pair of jockey shorts.

"Sir! You forgot these—"

Dr. Peters grabbed them, stuffing them into his bag as he strode down the windowed concourse toward the gates.

"I said, get your hands off her," Cole repeated in a steely tone. In front of him the security officer somewhat unsteadily stood his ground. "She's not a criminal. She's a doctor—a psychiatrist."

Kathryn shot him an alarmed look, turning as she heard a flurry of footsteps. A few yards away she recognized the bulky figure of Detective Dalva, several photos clutched in his hand. Behind him the airport detective brandished a walkie-talkie. Desperately she turned back to Cole and spotted Dr. Peters hurrying out of sight."

"THERE HE IS!" she shouted, pointing down the concourse. "THAT MAN! HE'S CARRYING A DEADLY VIRUS! STOP HIM!"

Cole whirled. He saw a ponytailed man hurrying down the hallway, looking back over his shoulder with a pinched, frightened face. A man with a ponytail and baggy plaid pants.

The man from his dream.

"PLEASE, SOMEBODY—STOP HIM!" Kathryn's voice rose to a shriek as Detective Dalva ran up beside her.

"Police officer," he gasped, flashing a badge. "Would you step over here, please?"

Before she could move Cole lunged at him,

knocking him off balance, then sprinted toward the magnetic arch and through it. With a deafening wail the alarm went off. People murmured, then cried out as the airport security officer dashed after him. Without looking aside Cole slammed his fist into him and sent him crashing to the floor. On the concourse fifty yards ahead, the ashen-faced Dr. Peters looked back to see James Cole yank a pistol from his pocket. On the ground the sprawling officer shouted, horrified.

"He's got a gun!"

Gasping, Cole sprinted up the concourse. Behind him a second security officer stood with legs apart, taking aim with his gun.

"Stop or I'll shoot!"

Cole raced on, heedless of terrified travelers screaming and diving for cover in his wake, heedless of the small boy standing before the observation window between his parents, watching in pure wonder as a 737 touched down upon the runway.

Another scream. Brow furrowed, the boy turned, and was knocked backward as a ponytailed man bumped into him.

"Watch it!" the man yelled.

The boy stared wide-eyed as the man clutched a Chicago Bulls gym bag to his chest, pirouetting gracelessly as he ran. An instant later a second man appeared: blond, wild-eyed, a mustache drooping ridiculously from his lip as he waved a pistol. Behind him lunged a uniformed man with another gun, aiming for the blond man as he angled through the crowded passageway.

"NOOOOO!"

As in a dream the boy turned, slowly, slowly. Up the hall raced a blond woman, her high heels nearly tripping her as she staggered forward desperately, her mouth thrown open in anguish. There was a *crack!*—a thousand thunderous echoes in the endless corridor. A few feet in front of the boy the blond man shuddered, staggered forward a few steps and then fell—falling, falling . . .

"My God! They've shot that man!"

His mother's voice, his mother's hand tightening on his shoulder. The boy stared, mesmerized, as the blond woman rushed up to the fallen man and knelt beside him. Across the gaudy tropical print crimson petals bloomed, stained the woman's hands as she leaned over him. So slowly he almost seemed not to move at all, the blond man lifted his hand. Tenderly he grazed the woman's cheek, touched her tears as she gasped and shook her head.

"Come on, son." His father pulled him away, gently but insistently, as airport medics ran up and pushed the woman aside, frantically trying to save the man. "This is no place for us."

As his father led him away, he looked back. The medics exchanged looks, shrugging helplessly. His father pulled him roughly toward a corner. His mother's hand nestled in his hair and he could hear her murmuring, more to herself than to him: "It's okay, don't worry, it's all going to be okay . . ."

But then and always and forever after, he knew that she was lying—nothing was ever going to be okay again. Even then, he knew he had watched a man die.

He slowed, not wanting to turn the corner, and looked back. Beside the dead man the blond woman staggered to her feet, her face streaked with tears. Quickly she turned and began scanning the crowd of onlookers, desperately searching for something. Two men in uniforms approached her, said something. The woman replied, her eyes still scanning the concourse. She looked around, distracted and unresisting, as the detectives handcuffed her. Suddenly, she froze.

And gazed directly at the boy.

He stared at her mutely, overwhelmed by her expression: love, but not what he had ever seen in his parents' eyes. Instead her eyes held a wild unruly thing that, even as he gazed back at her, he saw tamed, grow calm, even resigned, as though by looking at him she had somehow found some peace she had been frantically searching for.

"Hurry up, son."

With a last lingering look at her, the boy turned away. His eyes filled with tears and he began to cry, silently, as his mother ruffled his hair and murmured:

"Pretend it was just a bad dream, Jimmy."

At the entrance to Gate 38, the last few passengers boarded Flight 784 to San Francisco. In the first-class cabin, Dr. Peters swung his Chicago Bulls bag into the overhead luggage rack, then pulled the door shut and with a noisy sigh collapsed into his seat.

"It's obscene, all this violence, all the lunacy!" the passenger next to him exclaimed. "Shootings at airports now. You might say, *we're* the next endangered species!"

Smiling affably, Dr. Peters agreed. "I think you're right, sir. I think you've hit the nail right on the head."

Beside him, a courtly silver-haired gentleman wearing a business suit and one gold earring offered his hand congenially.

Once, James Cole would have recognized him as the astrophysicist from the future. But *that* James Cole was dead.

"Jones is my name," he said. There was a glint of very white teeth as he smiled. "I'm in insurance."

Moments later in the airport parking lot, a small boy stood and watched as a 747 climbed into the pale blue sky, higher and higher, until it winked like a tear from view.

✝

Elizabeth Hand is the author of *Waking the Moon*, *Winterlong*, *Æstival Tide*, *Icarus Descending*, and numerous short stories and plays. She lives in Maine with novelist Richard Grant and their two children.